Novus

The Corescu Chronicles Book Five

ellen c. maze

Novus
The Corescu Chronicles Book Five
By Ellen C. Maze
©2020 by Ellen C. Maze Sallas
All rights reserved.

ISBN: 9781734047486
Also in eBook
V.08172020

Cover photo / wings © Fernando Cortes – 123rf.com
Cover photo/man © curaphotography – 123rf.com
Cover Design: Elizabeth E. Little, Hyliian Design
Little Roni Publishers, LLC
www.littleronipublishers.com

Unless otherwise noted, Scripture is taken from the New King James Version®. Copyright © 1982 by Thomas Nelson. Used by permission. All rights reserved.

The following is a work of fiction. Names, characters, places, and incidents are fictitious or used fictitiously. Any resemblance to real persons, living or dead, to factual events or to businesses is coincidental and unintentional.

Let's stay in touch!
Enter your email address to join my newsletter. You'll receive exclusive deals and special offers, and be the first to know about new releases. *You can unsubscribe at any time.*
I included a free book!
https://dl.bookfunnel.com/z0c7dpe1am

PUBLISHED IN THE UNITED STATES OF AMERICA

Novus (NOE-voos)

Latin; new, fresh, unusual, strange, revived, unheard

NOVUS ~ a new beginning!
For a new vampire, that is everything.

Joseph Ellerslie watches the vampire magician with eyes as big as saucers. He wants to be amazing. He wants to live forever. Attending Law School and serving in his father's church had been a good plan, but a new future loomed. One filled with magic, mystery, and beautiful women. What he doesn't know is that his parents have sent a tenacious P.I. to bring him home, and worse, a local serial killer sets his eye on the boy with the white-blond hair…

Read the exciting and thrilling conclusion of *The Corescu Chronicles!*

Table of Contents

Prologue | The Runaways 1

1 | The Kissing Vampire 8

2 | The Private Investigator 18

3 | The Servant Heart 27

4 | The Reaper 30

5 | The Other Woman 37

6 | The Bossy Blonde American 42

7 | The Stalker 49

8 | The Trustworthy Servant 57

9 | The Obsession 63

10 | The Roustabout 79

11 | The Argument 86

12 | The Visitor 91

13 | The Hideaway 99

14 | The Little Orphan Boy 111

15 | The Sneak 120

16 | The Attack 129

17 | The Compromise 143

18 | The Letter 147

19 | The Decision 152

20 | The Lovers 154

Novel Excerpt | Rabbit: Chasing Beth Rider 159

Prologue[1] | The Runaways

Give no regard to mediums and familiar spirits;
do not seek after them, to be defiled by them:
I am the LORD your God.
Leviticus 19:31

"MAYBE YOU'RE JUST A HEDONIST," Joey said with a laugh and his friend rolled his head to the side.

"This is a big word. Do you know what it means?" Androni asked, his eyes flashing with humor.

With a dramatic exhale, Joey faced the dark ceiling, the two of them lying atop the hotel bed and hours away from escaping the country, leaving the dreary sad-sacks (as Androni called Tony and the doctor) behind forever. "I certainly do," he said in a sigh.

Androni chuckled deep in his throat and then also rolled his face to stare upwards. "I like to feel good and I like things that make me feel good."

Joey grinned at his friend's honesty. *"Yep, that's hedonism,"* he said barely audible. His vampire friend pretended not to hear.

"You make me feel good. I'm keeping you. You are *mine,"* he said with a definitive edge and rolled his face to Joey's profile. "I'm claiming you."

"You're claiming me," Joey said as a statement and also turned his face to meet the vampire's gaze. "Am I allowed to claim you back or is this some sort of *vampire master and his proselyte* thing?"

Androni's mouth formed a half grin and he looked

---

[1] *Pulled from Chapters 35 & 40 from Anathema, Book Four of The Corescu Chronicles, inserted here for anyone who needs a refresher of the end of that book.*

upwards again. "I'm making it up as we go. I have two centuries of figuring out what I like and don't like; of this I am an expert. Beyond that, I will wing it." He lifted his arms to prop behind his head still facing the ceiling. "We will figure it out together."

Joey mimicked his position and gave a nod. "Let the record show that I'm claiming you, too. You're mine."

Androni rolled onto his side to face Joey and rested his head into his hand. "I'm yours for what?" he asked, his gaze intense. "Blood? Mentoring? Companionship?"

"All that," Joey replied and also rolled onto his side. He had more to snark, but he met Androni's eyes and there it was; a breathless amazement that filled his mind when he locked onto the magician's face. He parted his lips, but no words emitted. As if from far away, Joey lifted his outside hand and moved a curl of black hair from his friend's forehead. Androni looked so *friendly,* so *open,* and his features rivaled those of any superstar on the movie screen. The vampire's eyes flashed in the low lighting and he smiled, moistening his lips as if knowing Joey would look there.

"Are you doing this?" Joey asked, a fuzz in his mind. It wasn't unpleasant, but it *was* foreign. "Are you hypnotizing me every time I look at your face?"

"No," Androni replied. "You love me all by yourself."

Joey grinned and returned to his earlier position, on his back and looking upwards. "That must be it. When I look at you, I'm *hopeful.* Everything's gonna be okay. I see a lot of good things ahead."

"I see the same thing," his friend offered in a quiet voice.

Joey had an idea. "You know about Doctor Corescu's partner, Paul. He told me that he loved him, and they had a really good life together for a hundred years. Have you had someone before me? Someone you wanted to claim?" Joey turned his face to find Androni had remained on his side, watching Joey's profile. As since they met, the man's attention was so intense and thoughtful. *Why?* he wondered inside; he'd never been so interesting to anyone in his life.

"No," he said at the same low volume. "The humans are food to me. You? I see you as a friend."

"The humans are food to me," he repeated in Androni's accent and chuckled. Since running off together, Androni had feasted on a few people, leaving them confused but alive and uninjured. So far, Joey had only taken blood from Androni. Would he really bite someone? Or could he skirt the activity by sticking to vampire blood?

"We must determine how Mark ruined our telepathy. I am unhappy about that. Very unhappy. Seeing your thoughts gave me great joy."

"Me, too," Joey replied, and met his eye. "You said we're going to your circus company. What then?"

"There, I play a Satanist with amazing, mystical dark powers. It is an act. But there is a sorceress who practices in earnest. I believe she can restore us. She has power. I have witnessed this."

Joey's scalp prickled at the thought of using witchcraft. His friend noticed the change and moved into a sitting position, cross-legged facing Joey lying down.

"You are afraid," he said, scrutinizing Joey's face.

"It's called holy fear," Joey said not expecting his friend to understand. And he didn't. Androni held the same expression and waited for more. Joey continued. "God abhors witchcraft. He said, do not seek out spiritists or mediums, you will be defiled by them." Joey shrugged one shoulder and put his palm to Androni's closest knee.

His friend nodded, incorporating his entire upper body, and covered Joey's fingers with his own. "You intend to maintain your religion?"

"Yeah." Joey couldn't lie; he wanted Jesus. He couldn't leave God no matter what. Would this shrink Androni's affection? Joey ran it down in his mind and his entire body rushed with emotion.

Androni growled. "I want to hear your thoughts!"

With drama and an audible *umph,* he fell onto his side against Joey, their bodies in contact all the way down.

"Your expression," he said in a kind whisper. "I hate it." He tucked one arm behind Joey's shoulders and the outside hand he put to his cheek and looked upon his face. "It is a look of fear, uncertainty, and distrust." Then Androni's arms encircled Joey with fervor, as if such an embrace would erase everything negative in their current discussion.

"I'm sorry," Joey said with meaning. "I don't want to make you upset. Honest."

"I wouldn't be upset if we had our telepathy returned. I wouldn't be upset if you ceased doubting my affection, my *commitment* to our union." Androni exhaled and finished in a whisper. *"I would be happy if you would dump this restrictive religion and allow ME to be your god."*

Joey's blood ran cold and in a reflexive move, his body tensed, and he shook his head no. He expected Androni to push away, leap from the bed, and disappear out the door forever. His eyes turned to the exit as the thought touched his mind.

Androni pulled him closer into his body, so now, Joey's cheek pressed to the magician's chest muscle. He held him there, rocking him like an infant, and then he whispered into Joey's hair, *"You will not have to choose, beloved Ghost."*

Ghost… Joey loved his new nickname and he loved it in his best friend's mouth.

"I would never make you choose." Androni kissed the top of his head. "I have claimed you from all flesh, humans and vampires. But as for God, I do not know

Him. He owns your spirit. I will share that part of my Ghost."

Joey exhaled staring at nothing, his mind thanking God, even though he hadn't had a reciprocating exchange in days. Androni kissed his hair again and moved to kiss his forehead, then his nose tip, and when he met Joey's eyes a moment, he rolled lower to kiss his mouth. Joey was learning to mimic his efforts and he wondered if maybe he was going to finally do it right. It still felt strange and it didn't come naturally, but it made his new friend so happy that Joey would keep trying.

…Roughly a month later…

"IT IS DONE."

Joey sat up from a light sleep, gasping for air. He stared at the dark space, his heart hammering and his ears popping. When he wiggled a thumb to the source of discomfort, a cool palm rubbed his back.

"We're not rising until dark. What are you doing?"

Joey slowed his breathing with effort and he swallowed hard. *Is the doctor dead?*

Androni sat up and grabbed his shoulder. "Did you just think *Mark is dead?*"

Joey whipped his eyes to Androni's. *"I think the doctor is dead,"* he sent as a thought.

Androni's face exploded into a grin and he leapt from the messy mattress to pound the caravan's metal ceiling. Then he stopped himself as if realizing what he had just heard. "Why do you think he's dead?"

Joey shook his head. "I don't know exactly. I had a chill and I heard in my head, *it is done.*" He narrowed his eyes in thought. "It sounded like the angel that helped me in the barn." He turned his gaze to his friend. "If it was, then I think God wants me to know that Doctor Corescu went home."

"He went home, eh? That is a romantic way of

saying someone died?" Androni asked in a laugh, but Joey wasn't offended. "Are you okay?" he asked.

Thinking over his reply, Joey looked out the tiny window into the late afternoon light. They had not contacted anyone from home in more than four weeks. Joey decided to let his parents think he ran away and maybe down the road he would send them a card. He didn't want them to worry but his dad expressed himself plainly the last time they talked—he despised all of the people associated with Pastor Tony.

Heck, I think he despises me, too.

The thought no longer hurt as it had a few weeks ago. Joey sighed; he did feel bad that the man was gone but they had not developed any sort of relationship in their time together. The doctor was frightening and knew it, using his supernatural superiority to cow Joey into submission in their every interaction.

"He is gone, no more mean vampires pestering my Ghost," Androni said low.

"Yeah," Joey replied and turned his face. Androni's eyes were filled with immense joy and his childlike expression brought Joey a new grin. "What?"

"Hearing your thoughts, oh, I have missed that!" he said and grabbed Joey to cover his face with kisses. Joey laughed at his exuberance but it would be an adjustment since he had fallen out of practice of guarding his thoughts.

Now he's going to know I don't want to bite anybody...

"Oh, beautiful boy!" Androni said and kissed both cheeks European style. "You will never have to do anything you do not wish to do. You are here to live! Remember what I told you, we will live! And that means you will be happy. I promise."

Joey received the affection and when his pal backed away, he thought again about the doctor. He did not know exactly what happened, but it was most likely that the doctor and Tony received the deliverance they desired. If that was true, it followed that Joey could as well; if he wanted to leave his new life, God would allow it.

Androni's expression fell and Joey surged close to take his shoulders. "I'm not going anywhere. I want to be with you. Let's do it, let's live."

Androni's smile returned and he collapsed onto the bed. "We will have a great life!" he said aloud and then he sent Joey a thought. *"I will show you how to do magic. We will wow the crowds with two magicians, the Ghost and the Gypsy. Oh, the adventures we will have."*

Joey recalled the ball flying through the air upon their first meeting and he grinned. What would God do if he stayed a while? Enjoyed his friend? Didn't the prosperity preacher Pastor Hawken say that God wanted His children to be happy and wealthy? Joey nodded to himself.

God will help me figure this out. I love Jesus and I love Androni.

His friend double-raised his eyebrows. "Ghost, my love, we will live!"

Joey agreed with a cheer believing they really would.

1 | The Kissing Vampire

Blessed is the man
Who walks not in the counsel of the ungodly,
Nor stands in the path of sinners,
Nor sits in the seat of the scornful;
But his delight is in the law of the Lord.
Psalm 1:1

"YOU WONDER WHY I KISS YOU," the magician said, and Joey huffed a nervous chuckle. "It is because only a vampire's mouth enjoys tactile sensation. Because of this, I put my lips on my favorite things."

"I guess that makes sense," Joey said in a nod.

Besides those areas, Joseph's body was numb. Since Haman Troye turned him into a bloodthirsty creature, Joey experienced tangible pressure, but no sensations of pain or pleasure. It truly felt as if his body had *gone to sleep,* like when he slept on his arm or when the dentist applied lidocaine before filling a cavity. In contrast, the nerve endings of Joey's lips, palate, gums, and tongue were more sensitive than ever.

"At first, I thought maybe you were gay," Joey offered with a soft laugh and looked into the night sky. They had opted for a moonlight stroll and the air was alive with the sound of crickets and owls.

"Hah, yes," his friend said in a huff. "You have figured out by now that sexual preference loses its meaning as a vampire."

Joey blushed at the topic and Androni gave a soft chuckle. His friend had shared an overview of his past. He started out as *Androni Miklos,* a man with a wife who worked on enormous farms doing all manner of trades.

Tragedy struck when mere weeks into the marriage, a group of roving pillagers stole his wife and kidnapped him, only to toss as a snack to their pet monster the following evening. The creature in the cave transformed Androni into a vampire and disappeared, leaving him to figure out the vampire's life on his own.

They strolled slowly, both in thought, and Joey looked over to consider Androni's handsome face. On its own accord, his heart sent thanks to God that the magician survived and stood at his side.

I know Androni is the reason I haven't gone insane with this weird and scary trial…

"Come here," Androni said and pulled him close with one arm. Being taller, he held Joey against his chest and spoke over his hair. "I think I am using our embraces to affirm my life, even more so than your delicious blood."

"I like the sound of that," Joey returned. No matter what Androni said about him, the sentiment was always more positive than anyone had ever shared before. Joey chuckled then, his body wrapped snug to his friend. Androni leaned out to see his face. "I was just thinking what a horrible kisser I am. I'll get better. I promise."

"Nothing about you is horrible. You must know this by now. You have become everything to me. I will never let you go."

"I feel exactly the same way," Joey whispered, touched at the devotion.

Androni resumed the embrace. "Thank you for running away with me," he whispered over Joey's head.

"Thank you for wanting me along," Joey replied and held tight.

They stood together in the cool night air, trees and forest greenery pressing in on all sides, the canopy revealing half of the sky. Joey had never been happier. He sighed and did not let go for a very long time.

The next morning, the weatherman promised rain; the skies were gray, and the sun remained hidden. Joey rose first as usual and jogged to Eli's trailer. At his back door, the man handed Joey two rolled-up newspapers. Androni never gave out his address, so Eli stood in whenever such was needed. The Polish roustabout, as Joey learned early on, was the only person at the circus that Androni liked, much less trusted. The man was thick with a bushy beard and eyebrows that met over a bulbous nose. How old was he? Joey would guess mid-fifties but when asked, Androni had no idea. It didn't matter; the man took care of whatever the magician needed, and two mornings a week, that meant collecting their newspapers.

When Joey returned to the caravan, his friend had moved to the sofa, and met his eye with one hand open. Joey shot him a grin, lobbed the paper, and sat against him with an oomph.

Two vampires reading the news, Joey mused, and it was fifteen minutes before either of them spoke. Androni broke the silence.

"I'm hungry," he said low. He had been leaning against Joey as he read, but he straightened and dropped a palm to Joey's upper back. "Who shall we eat tonight, Ghost? The new stable boy?" he asked in a silly warble, his palm making small circles across Joey's shoulder blades. He enjoyed the sensation. It didn't feel like it would have before his transformation, but he cherished the closeness. Then the hand was gone.

"Don't stop," Joey said, his eyes on his English-language newspaper. "Tell me more about how hungry you are," Joey said with snark. It was hours *and hours* before they would eat, and he enjoyed this new tradition of listening to Androni whine in his beautiful Hungarian accent.

"You like my voice, little Ghost?" Androni asked and returned to rubbing his back. "Then I will repeat for you this truth: I am glad you're here. I have never been happier than this moment."

"Me, too," Joey agreed.

They had been at Androni's circus company for a month and both enjoyed this quiet time, side-by-side, Joey reading the *U.S.A. Journal* and Androni the local *Caller*. As old-fashioned as it was to read the news in print, Joey had destroyed his iPhone to avoid his parents. Now he lived as Androni always had—off the grid, which meant no smart phones and no internet.

"Did you see anything of interest to vampire magicians in that snazzy paper?"

Joey huffed a short laugh. "Nothing. How about yours?"

"There is a curfew in effect until they catch The Reaper." His friend had spoken while reading and his hand fell still on Joey's back.

Two weeks ago, the media so-named a local killer and now it would seem the police were getting desperate. The nearest village was a tiny hamlet nestled in the forest, home to a hundred souls, but the closest city boasted twenty thousand and this was where the killings occurred.

"The Reaper," Androni repeated. He folded his paper closed. "I wonder if we might find him. How would we do that? Hunt down a killer?" He turned to Joey, truly asking.

"Umm, I guess we'd need to know everything the police have on the guy and go from there. Know anyone in the *polizei*?" Joey asked, enjoying the use of the foreign word. Androni grinned, holding his eye, as always looking like a man who enjoyed his friend very much.

"No, no *polizei* at the circus," Androni teased saying the word poorly on Joey's account. "On winter break, let us nose about. We will go on holiday."

"Take a vacation," Joey corrected, Americanizing his phrase.

In three weeks, The Company, as Androni called his circus, would pack up and travel south for the winter. The ringmaster begged Androni to come, but for as long as he had been in the man's show, he never traveled with them in the winter, preferring to spend the off time sneaking about the various settlements for adventure. This season, perhaps they would turn his friend's amazing mind to finding a killer. Could be interesting.

"Aren't there six more performances until the break?" Joey asked and Androni gave him a nod. "Okay. If they don't catch The Reaper by then, let's do it. I bet you could teach me some cool stuff about sneaking around."

Androni made no response and Joey looked over. "What are you thinking? I can't understand what I'm hearing in your head." His friend's thoughts were often in another language and as he waited, the magician grinned.

"You will learn more about your Gypsy as time passes, but I have lived a quiet life. The vampires you've met—Haman, Mark—they have lived much more aggressively." Androni's tone had turned wistful and his gaze soft. "As a youth, I abhorred fisticuffs and any sort of brutality. I learned how to avoid punishment and my guardians found me to be a very compliant ward."

Joey listened at rapt attention, loving the story, Androni's voice, the… everything. Androni grinned at his transmitted thoughts and continued.

"I grew up strong and capable, but clever enough to avoid aggression in all its forms. When I awoke a vampire, I discovered within a month that I could take my fill of blood without violence. So you and I will seek out this killer, learning together how to stalk and overcome such an animal among man." He waggled his eyebrows. "This would be a fun hobby over the winter break, eh?"

"Yeah…" Joey turned his gaze to the caravan's

small window. He and Androni had that in common, that his entire life, Joey had also avoided confrontation. Before the attack, he had sought his parents' approval in every aspect of his life. He pondered the next few days and weeks. Androni wanted him to join the show, perform together, but so far, Joey had begged off. His entire life he had been shy and self-conscious. In this respect, Androni was his complete opposite, enjoying the adulation and exposure the stage provided. Joey hoped to learn to be more like his friend and much less pensive and speculative about every tiny thing.

And learning together...

That was a fun notion. Being with Androni was a stark contrast to his time with the other vampires he'd met—Pastor Tony and Doctor Corescu. He had spent only an hour or so with Tony Agricola before the man was whisked away, entering seclusion where he prayed to be delivered of the vampire curse. Joey frowned, not ready to take his mind there. He considered the doctor, Mark Corescu, exuding power, wisdom, and a haughtiness that brought Joey more fear than peace. At one point, in an attempt to press a point, the doctor had grabbed Joey close and pretended to attack him. Joey had been scared witless.

All I wanted was to learn how to be as powerful as he was...

Androni nudged his arm. "His blood is inside you," he said low. "With concentration, you could multiply that vestige and grow your power."

Joey swiveled his face, close as they sat together on the small couch. "Really?"

"Sure." Androni dropped his journal to the floor at his heel.

Joey also set his paper down, his mind putting science to the metaphysical elements of vampirism. If Haman put the doctor's blood into his veins (as Joey had heard it went), then Haman became a vampire from that transfer. Haman must have put his blood into Joey's veins when he was unconscious, which is why he awoke a vampire. He looked to Androni. "Why haven't you made other vampires?"

"I didn't know how," he replied without pause. He tipped his chin to Joey. "I can't read it all—what are you thinking about?"

"I was unconscious when Haman made me this way, but Pastor Tony told me that Haman was transformed by pouring the doctor's blood directly into his open veins. It was a blood transfusion that did it."

Androni lifted his brow with a nod. "Interesting."

Joey fell silent, his mind continuing the investigatory trail. Androni bumped his knee. "And?"

Joey grinned. "I was thinking that if the doctor's power is in me and you think it's his blood that is the key..." Joey gave a little shrug. "What happens if I somehow put *your* blood directly into my veins? If it makes a mortal into a vampire, would it serve to make a vampire more vampir-y? Would it make it easier for me to do magic? To be like you instead of like Doctor Corescu and Haman?"

Androni inhaled with interest. "Let us try. We have no restrictions."

Joey nodded but rolled in his lips. He was asking to go deeper into a curse his previous mentors suggested he avoid.

Androni made a *tsk* noise. "You said your God has been there thousands of years. He is not leaving tonight. Here. Give me your arm."

Joey offered an uneasy chuckle but did as Androni asked. His friend brandished a pocketknife while looking at the veins in Joey's wrist, figuring a way to proceed.

"I slice mine and yours and press them together?" he confirmed lifting his compelling gaze. Joey's stomach flopped as it so often did when he dove into his friend's eyes. Androni's dark hair and swarthy complexion were

14

enough to give him the ideal "vampire magician" appearance.

"I wonder if it will make me look like you," Joey said with a waggle of his eyebrows. "And I could use some of your charm."

Androni peeked up with a sideways grin. "Oh, no, my beautiful Ghost. You can be like Androni inside, but never change your appearance. Looking at you gives me the greatest joy in the world. More than blood. More than life."

Joey huffed, dropping his eyes back to the operation zone. "Teach me to talk like that. You always say the most romantic things."

"I will teach you everything I know," Androni said in a silky whisper and laid the sharp tip to his own forearm. "I will do it now."

He pressed the knife in a quarter inch and immediately moved it to Joey's inner arm to do the same. Without delay, they pressed their wounds together and looked into each other's eyes, sitting close, their faces inches apart.

"One, two, three, four, five," Joey counted in a whisper, grinning at how handsome his friend was so close. *"Seven, eight…* Oh!" Joey's brain fuzzed and then his heart seemed to expand in his ribcage. "Something's… happening," he said, alarmed at the new sensations. His eyes fell shut as pressure zoomed up his spinal column to rest at the base of his skull.

"Hah, my beloved, be still," Androni said in a rasp, feeling something on his end by the sound. Joey's eyes were still closed, but he felt his friend's free hand lift to cup his shoulder. Then the contact of their inner arms dropped and Androni grasped the other shoulder as well. As they were sitting, the motion twisted them both to a ¾ facing position. "Relax and let it come. Relax…"

Eyes still closed, Joey nodded, consciously commanding his mind to stop racing, stop worrying, stop tearing down whatever was happening. Androni's blood raced back down, leaving his head and neck and chest, he felt a pulse of nourishment flow to his toes before it filtered away. With an enormous exhale, he opened his eyes.

"Whoa," he whispered.

His friend grinned, his eyes smiling. "Your blood is making me want to drive fast cars," he teased.

"I feel different," Joey said in a serious tone. "I wonder if I am different."

"Oh, you are," his friend cooed and pulled him close to kiss his forehead. "The Gypsy's nose knows all." He laughed one chortle at his own joke and got to his feet.

Joey stood too, still waiting to "feel" something. Anything. Maybe it would take multiple hits. Maybe it would take time. He didn't want to frown, but he had wanted to feel *something…*

"Don't pout, beautiful Ghost," Androni teased, peering into his face when he looked up. "Close your eyes."

Joey did so and his friend cupped both cheeks. He expected a kiss, but instead, Androni did nothing for several moments. Then he said very softly, "An easy one, you will see my past. Look… I am thinking of my youth. What do you see?"

Joey's brain told him this was impossible, but he did indeed begin to receive images that were not his own memories. Behind closed lids, he watched two boys wrestling. The edges of the vision were hazy and monochromatic, but the center was as vivid as any of Joey's own thoughts. One of the boys shouted in fun. Joey didn't know the language, but he watched on, a grin hitting his mouth. Then the boys broke apart, facing each other, both black-haired and swarthy like his friend. The shorter of the two looked his way, Joey assumed—to Androni in this memory—and said something else. In his ear, his friend translated in a whisper, *"He is saying I should join them, but I did not enjoy rough-housing…"*

Then, in a sudden movement, the boys split apart, arms at their sides, as if trying to appear they hadn't been in contact. From behind Joey's vantage, a woman in white circumvented his position only to grasp both boys roughly by the ear. She faced Androni and spoke harshly before striding away, boys in hand. The memory faded and Joey opened his eyes.

"Was that a nurse?" Joey asked aware his friend was an orphan. "Were those your friends?" He sought his friend's eye as he awaited a reply. One, two, three long seconds, Androni swam in Joey's gaze, holding him in place as surely as with steel bonds. Then, with a debonair smile, he backed two steps and clasped his hands at his chest.

"More importantly… who shall we eat tonight, Ghost? Your Gypsy is so very hungry."

Joey grinned at the put-on mysterious timbre of his deep voice.

"The Ghost has blood," he said mimicking the sound. This made Androni's grin widen and Joey loved him more than ever. "Perhaps the Gypsy will sink his fangs into the Ghost's throat. Doesn't this sound fabulous?" Joey watched Androni's face, trying a new game, one that was bolder and could lead to embarrassment if his pal didn't play along. But he did.

"I *vant* to *drink* your *blood!*" he said in a vibrato reminiscent of Bela Lugosi's Dracula. And with a new grin, he pulled Joey close and found his favorite spot, just below the ear. He punched through and his arms wrapped Joey up tight.

Joey held his breath, but happy to be held close. It didn't hurt and very soon, they would turn the tables and Joey would feast. It had become a good game.

2 | The Private Investigator

Now therefore, be wise, O kings;
Be instructed, you judges of the earth.
Serve the Lord with fear
And rejoice with trembling.
Psalm 2:10-11

"WE WANT OUR BOY BACK!" Reverend Robert Ellerslie barked at volume when Andy asked him again to state his goals. He shoved a slim file folder toward Andy's chest. "Take this. Goldenblue already did the legwork."

Andy received the folder nodding. He had been the Ellerslie's second P.I., the first, a friend from his Academy days, refused to leave the country. He had mentioned the job to Andy offhandedly, not expecting anything, but Andy had his own reasons for getting involved. He watched the father's red face and concentrated on the task at hand.

"Everything's in there. Goldenblue traced Joseph's credit card, every stop from here to Hartsfield-Jackson. Stores, gas stations, hotels—dear God!" he exclaimed and glanced toward his wife before lowering his voice. *"Hotels! With that freak!"*

"Bob," the man's wife began but he quieted her with a hiss.

"He cleaned out his bank account. These places have cameras. Start there. Get my boy back and I don't care what you do to that whack-job Androni-whatever-his-name-is!"

"Wait now, Bob, let's be nice," Mrs. Ellerslie offered but her husband barreled on.

"Nice is done, JoAnn! We were so nice that a bunch

of tricksters sucked our boy into a cult!" Ellerslie wrung his palms and faced Andy. "Go get my boy! I'll pay whatever it costs."

Andy offered a serious nod watching the wife touch her husband's arm. He jerked out of reach and left the room, his cell coming to his ear. The woman turned to Andy, her face apologetic.

"I'm sorry for Bob, he's just scared, you know. We're both so worried." Andy nodded and left it at that. "How are you doing? Kent said you have a son with Down's. Is he doing well?" she asked, her eyes soft.

Andy gave her a genuine smile. Kent Goldenblue knew Billy from way back. The boy was grown and in a special home for adults with Down's. He was happy, but Andy admitted the house had grown lonely without him. *Which is probably why I got my private investigator's license after retirement. It was simply too quiet…*

To the woman he answered with a thank you, "Billy's tip-top. I suspect he'll be getting a promotion at work soon. If you go to the tavern, ask for him. He's becoming a favorite."

The woman said she would and Andy fell into his thoughts, both of them awaiting the return of Mr. (ahem, *Reverend* Ellerslie). Andy had been raised Andrew Jackson Kranchez, the third born of three sons to his mother, a staunch Presbyterian. And although his father rarely attended Sunday service, both parents expected their children to grow up in the church. Andy left as soon as allowed, which meant, as soon as he moved away.

Maybe I could use that pastor's help with this, Andy thought, his mind returning to the other side of this investigation coin. Anthony Agricola, the man who arrived at Bob Ellerslie's home, asked to see their son, and then whisked him away. By the couple's description, he had gone voluntarily, but his glazed expression and refusal to meet their eyes gave them plenty of suspicion.

Follow that up with soon afterward, the couple couldn't convince Joseph over the phone to return and they drove to Agricola's address in order to bring him by force. There again, the boy refused to comply. Although Agricola had not been present that night, Ellerslie shared how Doctor Corescu and the "crazy-looking European" followed him to his car and threatened him to leave.

Andy humphed. He'd been to Agricola's Montgomery home. He'd seen horrible things... His mind jumping tracks, he recalled that night he had accepted a call on the report of a break-in. What he saw could not be explained, then or now.

What had he seen? A tall commanding presence grasping their suspect by the upper arms. Andy watched as the stranger lifted his face from a raw wound in the suspect's throat. Didn't Andy see...

Did I see fangs dripping blood in the tall man's mouth?

Then, in a blink, the man was gone. How was that possible?

He was there, and then he was gone!

Andy shivered.

Maybe he hadn't been there. I was tired. Working long hours. Maybe I was just spooked by all the stuff Jenn and I were researching. I could have imagined it all...

Andy truly wished he imagined it. He and Jennifer Speltz-Miller investigated bloodless bodies all over the tri-county area the weeks leading up to this night. They were calling it a cult, but didn't they both think it might be true? That there were vampires loose in town?

Andy shook his head and cursed inside, happy Mrs. Ellerslie (ahem, also *Reverend*) remained quiet. He didn't think his voice would be calm should she engage him in chit chat.

For the sake of his current investigation, Andy decided maybe the tall stranger *hadn't* been there. This played so much better from every angle. After all, the tall man who appeared to be Doctor Mark Corescu, disappeared in such a way that the suspect in his grip did not drop when the apparition was gone. Instead, the perp remained standing and swiveled a monstrous face toward Bailey on Andy's left. When the suspect named Rakha Tep opened his mouth, reality took another hit: Andy saw *teeth*. Not doggish canines, but *rows* of teeth, top and bottom, sharp as knives and ready to bite. Tep's mouth had then opened impossibly wide below eyes that shone red. Tep surged into the junior man, grabbing his upper arms. Not with fingers ending in sharp nails, but *phalanges* from the wrist out, glimmering like metal and sharp as knives. *What was this thing?* Was it a man in special effects makeup?

In that moment, Andy's mind had traveled two tracks—reality (it must be a trick of the light) and Jenn's bloodless bodies research (it is an honest-to-God vampire!).

But no way. It couldn't be. During the next few seconds, the questionable light from the hallway tossed confusion on a scene Andy would never forget.

Pouncey, the officer to Andy's right, had the presence of mind to call out, "Freeze! Don't move! Put your hands where I can see them!"

At the command and in a blur of movement the suspect attacked, latching his vicious mouth (if it had been as Andy saw it) into the officer's throat. Bailey screamed for help as Pouncey raised his weapon.

"Crossfire! Crossfire!" the man shouted and emptied his weapon into Tep's upper body.

Seemingly unaffected, the suspect continued to ravage Bailey's throat and Andy's fugue broke. With his trigger finger in place, he also emptied his magazine into the killer who did not cease his movement until Andy dry-fired. His partner had reloaded, and as their compatriot was dropped lifeless to the floor, the suspect went to his knees, facing Andy and Pouncey.

And he wasn't dead. Not by a long shot.

Andy stared into the perp's impossible movie-makeup face and ejected his mag for a reload. Slamming it home, he lifted the barrel to eye level. He stood fifteen feet from where Tep knelt on the Agricola's hardwood floor, but the guy made no move. Instead, he simply stared up at them, blackish blood oozing from innumerable entry wounds, a gurgling sound issuing from chest wounds that must have punctured lungs, and reddish air bubbles emitting from the thing's mouth.

The thing.

This was real. This was happening. Andy did the only thing he could. With part of his mind counting the boots of his backup rumbling up the stairs, he aimed one last time, forehead-center, and pulled. Tep went down, slumping to the side, cheek to the floor, dead rag-doll arms crooked before him, bent knees limp as noodles. He was dead. *It* was dead.

Andy and Pouncey had stepped to the dead man, peering down as if studying an insect. It didn't look human. Its eyes were at half-mast but open, silvery red orbs running watery fluid tinged red. The skin on his face was stretched tight making his eyes appear enormous, even when mostly closed. That mouth full of teeth was half-open in its dead state, and Andy could not deny they were indeed like that of a piranha. What was Pouncey thinking? Would he ever ask? No, it was more likely both of them would enter a report that did NOT include what they were looking at. They would smooth it over for the record. Whatever he was, he was dead and gone. The unexplainable stuff would not go in anything Andy wrote. The end.

But the sight of that monster's face and the aroma of his brains seeping onto the homeowner's bedroom floor had never left Andy's memory. Andy shivered anew. It was over. Happened more than a month ago. He had retired soon after. He was done. He'd put in his years. He was going to be okay. But that image – the teeth, the eyes, the claws – haunted him. This is why he took Robert Ellerslie's call. He had to prove to himself that he hadn't seen all that. His "monster-suspect", Rakha Tep, was mixed up with Agricola, who was mixed up with Mark Corescu, who was mixed up with the European, and all of them knew Joseph Ellerslie. Because Andy knew about Tep, wasn't he responsible to help when asked?

Andy did not attend church anymore, but he believed God was involved with His people's everyday lives. He believed in predeterminism, that if he did the best he could in all things, he'd find God determined his ending from Creation. This faith gave him comfort in his law enforcement career and now? It would help him as he pondered impossible mythical creatures and their effect on an innocent local teenager.

When Jenn requested his help, mostly asking for use of the LE database, Andy jumped in admittedly to spend time with his friend's sexy now-wife. Jonah Miller hadn't wanted to play, so he and Jenn worked it alone, digging up file after file of bloodless bodies in the tri-county area connecting them to the members of what Andy now considered a possible Satanic cult. Most of the evidence traced to Doctor Mark Corescu and his now-deceased accomplice (un-charged) Paul Black.

Mark Corescu.

Andy exhaled, trying not to draw Mrs. Ellerslie's attention. She was still off in her thoughts, gazing at her phone.

But the doctor.

If Andy indeed saw Corescu "biting" Rakha Tep, did that make this a vampire battle? Like in a Hollywood movie? Following the train of thought, did that make Tep Corescu's subordinate? This could explain the nightmarish face on the suspect.

I mean, dang! Jonah got bit in the neck by this Tep character!

He never said anything about vampires!

No, his old friend insisted the man was insane, not supernatural.

But would I do that too? Didn't I? No cop would ever file a report with the boogey man in it.

Today, Mark Corescu was off the grid. Andy could find him nowhere. Had he returned to Europe with the Ellerslie kid? Andy had questioned Agricola, a known associate of the doctor from Whitford City and come up empty.

And Jonah's daughter was dating Corescu! Doesn't that make him okay? Jonah wouldn't trust him if he was a monster. It didn't add up and Andy huffed.

Then there's Speltz!

When Andy asked her about the doctor, she had no idea who he was. She had no memory of any of the dozens of hours they spent together researching the guy. The day he asked about it, Jonah caught them talking and interrupted, changing the subject. Later, he asked Andy in private to not bring it up again.

He wouldn't, but… the look in her eyes…

She had no idea what I was talking about!

How can a woman as brilliant as detective Jennifer Speltz *not* remember? It did not make sense.

Unless, vampires were real and one of them hypnotized her to forget.

Andy chuckled with a shake of the head; he had officially entered the twilight zone. The *crazy* zone. It was time to get some perspective, time to rename everything before he lost his mind.

Taking a deep breath, Andy labeled the participants as cult members. Mark Corescu as the possible leader, suspected members were Paul Black, the European, Anthony Agricola (a.k.a. Pastor Tony), maybe his wife…

Andy rolled his eyes; Sarah Tracey Agricola had been viciously attacked by Paul Black in a parking lot before he ever got involved with bloodless bodies. That was a year ago, when Jonah and Jenn were seeking POI's for a case in Whitford City of a dead journalist out of Kentucky. Oh, how the lines tied, he'd need a pen and paper to sort them out.

Bob Ellerslie reentered the room with purpose and gave Andy a steely gaze. "That was my guy at the bank. Agricola deposited money in my boy's account." His eyes flashed with anger, maybe even hatred, which spooked Andy since the guy was the pastor of the city's largest evangelical church. "I'm warning you, don't trust Tony Agricola. Do not fall for that *I love Jesus* schtick. Have you seen his house? Do you see the way he lives? He has no income and lives like a king on that ridiculous estate. He is *crooked* and the cult is paying for it all! This is the way cults work. Goldenblue said that ass Mark Corescu owns property across Europe. Thousands of acres in assumed names and corporations. That's crooked, too! Not only that, his family name goes back generations. His wealth cannot be measured because he's as crooked as Agricola! Crooked!"

Andy nodded during Ellerslie's lecture, but he would reserve judgment. He liked Tony. Jonah did, too. If Tony Agricola was a devil, as Bob Ellerslie asserted, Andy and Jonah were horrible judges of character. This could not be true since between them, they had more than seventy years on the job reading suspects and interviewees. It was more likely Ellerslie was simply frightened for his boy, Andy would be, too, and he gave him grace on that account. Andy would be cautious when dealing with Agricola, but he also would trust his instincts. Many times, his gut feeling saved his skin and solved more cases than hard evidence did in all of his years on the force.

Agricola's behavior is suspicious, but he's no devil.

Andy never wanted to go into the ministry but he had a sense of justice, a desire to fight evil and protect the innocent that caused him to gravitate to law enforcement. His naturally gruff demeanor and size (he stood 6'3" and maintained a hefty if not slightly heavy weight) allowed him to assert himself with ease.

"I'm sure you are aware that the company you keep defines the man. Jesus teaches us to beware who we make friends with. Agricola is surrounding himself with known agitators if not flat-out killers! Goldenblue found police reports—Corescu's accomplice may have murdered a journalist in Georgia!"

He's never going to shut up, Andy thought as Ellerslie began a new rant, but held his face static. He wanted the job and angering the client wouldn't serve him well. *But I disagree here... the company Tony keeps doesn't necessarily define him.*

This was indeed a legitimate Bible precept, but everything wasn't always black and white. Andy himself had friends on the fringe, drug addicts, *sex* addicts, people he genuinely cared about, liked, and enjoyed their company. He stayed in their lives in order to be there for them when they needed his help. Andy didn't want to reach the pearly gates and have the Lord say, *"Belser called and you wouldn't pick up the phone. You got tired of him going back to jail over and over, you grew weary of his constant and frequent arrests, and how many times he ended up in the hospital with a drug overdose. The only number in his pocket was yours and you didn't answer the phone..."*

No way did Andy want the Lord to say to him, "When I was hungry, you didn't feed me, when I was in prison, you didn't visit me..." This teaching from Andy's childhood remained and had become part of his being. He would investigate, he would find the boy and bring him home, but he would reserve judgment. What if Tony Agricola is only trying to help the boy in some way? Help this doctor and this weird guy from Europe?

He would do his job and trust God to know the ending.

3 | The Servant Heart

Lead me, O Lord, in Your righteousness because of my enemies;
Make Your way straight before my face.
Psalm 5:8

"YOU HAVE TO GO. YOU KNOW THAT, RIGHT?"

Tony gave his wife a nod, aware that with the Ellerslies' constant calling and his own inner worry, they needed to check on Joseph in person. The thing that Tony didn't like so much was that Sarah felt like he needed to go alone, that Tony needed to go to Europe and leave her behind.

"There's no other way? The Lord won't let you go with me?"

"No," she said, her tone sorrowful. "I have had three visions and they all come up with the same interpretation: I have to stay here. Something huge is on the horizon and I want to believe it's Joey coming home and Androni finding Jesus. God won't show me the end, but I will pray for all three of you."

She gave Tony a smile that melted his heart and he pulled her into a hug. Taller by inches she kissed his head and spoke into his hair.

"You know this is all going to work out for God's purposes, right? You know that no matter what, He has our backs."

Tony nodded and squeezed, feeling frisky holding her so close. Now that the vampire curse had been lifted off his spirit, he and Sarah were able to enjoy the marriage bed, where before as a vampire, he had no sensation to make it work. On top of that, the Lord healed her malformed uterus; despite her doctor's predictions, she experienced no pain in their lovemaking. Before they were wed, she advised him she was a virgin and that her doctor had warned her internal conformation rendered her infertile. Being barren was not an issue as they were both happy leaving such things to the Lord, but Tony did not want to hurt her in any way. He had only one girlfriend before Sarah and now, by the Lord's grace, was truly enjoying what the Lord provided in the way of man and wife intimacy. Tony growled a little sound that she would recognize and she giggled.

"Now, now, Pastor Tony. It's 10 o'clock in the morning. None of that huggle-bear stuff…"

Tony ignored her and growled again, this time opening his palms to her long back. He slid his hands to her waist and pulled back to look into her face. "Do you have an appointment, Mrs. Agricola?" he asked with a grin.

She met his eye and shook her head. "We were talking about how to help Joey and Androni."

Tony kissed her nose. "Well, I reserve the right to re-approach this matter." With a swipe to her behind he led his wife to the dinette where they each sat. "What is the latest news from JoAnn?" he asked and sipped his iced tea.

The boy's parents had hired a detective they knew from their congregation to track down their son. Then Joey left the country and they handed it to a cop Tony knew from his Paul Black days, Andy Kranchez.

Having Kranchez involved gave Tony concern because he could possibly be aware of vampires. When he and Mark were trying to destroy Rakha, Kranchez had been first on the scene. Mark confided to Tony that the man may have seen him biting Rakha and may have seen him disappear. Tony extrapolated from there that if he saw all that, then he would have seen the demon's true visage—the pale taut skin and gaping mouth full of sharp teeth. Tony had seen it. Kranchez would never forget that. Tony couldn't know any of this for sure. He had asked Jonah if his cop-friend confided anything of it to him, but he had not. In fact, Jonah kept all of it from his wife to protect her from remembering anything about vampires and the bloodless bodies she had diligently and expertly researched.

Sarah refilled her tea glass and told him everything Joseph's mother reported most recently. The boy left the country and stopped using his credit card, his debit card, and his phone went dark. "Is Mark's friend Hope still in Germany? Maybe she would help find him," Sarah added at the end.

Tony only made a small noise of agreement. Hope Brannen had been *his* friend first. Along the way, she met Mark, fell for him hard, and because of the way God worked it, dragged Tony into the current vampire saga. Would she help if he asked? They hadn't spoken since Mark died. He and Sarah wrote her a condolence card to tell her (in code, in case it was opened) what happened with their doctor vampire friend. She hadn't responded. She had Tony's number and address, but had not reached out.

Would she help them find Joey?

Probably not. But the light in Sarah's eyes remained hopeful and as they closed out the topic, he moved in for a kiss. Time to return to the "huggle-bear stuff" and he smiled.

4 | The Reaper

For there is no faithfulness in their mouth;
Their inward part is destruction;
Their throat is an open tomb;
Psalm 5:9

THE UNFORTUNATE TIMING OF THE KILL forced Carle to keep the tailor's son on ice two days. This was not a problem; he'd long ago installed a chest freezer in the private office. It sported a sturdy lock and easily fit the corpse hidden beneath fake boxes of fish. It was Carle's personal office, his freezer, his lock—no one would bother it. No one bothered with him at all, and that was the way he preferred it. Friday, when the window of opportunity opened to dispose of the corpse in the Werra River, Carle did so, weighting it down and making sure it went to the bottom.

Ten, that had been his goal; bring ten laughing boys to the end of their lives, one for each year Carle faced without his father.

"Hi, Carle!" a young woman called as she passed his position. It was the American. He gave her less than a glance, finding the mere word, "American," irritated him to the core. None of the riders interested him. None of them were laughing boys. Instead, the equestrian center he ran for his family was home to three dozen Olympic level steeds and their spoiled rotten riders. Carle hated horses and hated the rich—although he had been wealthy his entire life. He didn't fit in, so he counted himself outside. He returned to daydreaming. He spent long days in the barn office, answering phones and shuffling papers, but no one expected him to be productive; his family hired people to do that. Carle kept an office at the equestrian center his family owned because he needed a place to think, a safe, dry, and warm place to plot and plan his revenge.

But I'm done, right? Ten. Ten laughing boys.

He searched inside, his eyes trained blindly to the large arena where the young women trotted their ridiculously expensive warmbloods around the ring. Ten didn't do it. He had no peace. His anger remained. Maybe he had the wrong number. Maybe he needed to kill a few more. Get a few more boys to pay for what their sort did to his father, Benedict Carle Waltershausen, the richest man in the state of Thuringia, Germany.

Benedict Waltershausen...

Carle considered his father. He hadn't been good at sharing his feelings or speaking of his woes, but he took good care of his family. And he hadn't inherited the family fortune as most of the village believed. Benedict's family disowned him very young for choosing the wrong political party. After the war, he bought and resold property until up to his death, he was the most well-known landowner in the country. When he was murdered, as the oldest son, Carle discovered that his father was worth enough to purchase his parents' holdings several times over.

But he was murdered...

How a billionaire was beaten to death by teenagers in downtown Frankfort was something only Carle understood. A closet alcoholic himself, only Carle was aware of his father's weakness for fine bourbon consumed in secret. Benedict confided in Carle one evening when he was arrested for shouting at police. When they recognized his status, they quietly called his oldest son to pick him up and whisk him home. Carle had done so and for seven years, he never told a soul. But since he knew, his father revealed to his son when he left and when he returned. Having such a secret between them felt nice, made Carle feel special. Along the way, Carle learned his father gravitated toward the lower-end establishments, rough and dirty—not for women—but to soak up the seedy atmosphere in disguise. It was because of his disguises that he was killed.

On that fateful night, Benedict Waltershausen left his Realty office and ducked into a petrol station loo to don his shabby costume. He joined the crowds at his favorite pubs and by midnight, stumbled into a back alley, presumably to vomit. This is where the laughing boys found him, teased him, perceived his dress as a homeless man and proceeded to beat him with sticks and clubs. One boy laughed shrill and high as he swung a baseball bat at his father's temple. All of this was recorded by the boys who posted it soon after on social media. By the time the platform removed it from view, thousands of people had saved it to their devices. It would play over the internet and go viral for six weeks. Carle could not escape the horrific images even if he wanted to, because one of the boys—and he couldn't know which one—emailed it to the equestrian center once they learned the dead man owned it.

But I got those boys. All six of them.

It had taken only a month's research, but Carle located every boy from that night, each laughing mouth was silenced forever. And he clubbed them to death. He had to. In order to get justice for his father. The first laughing boy was killed in a field behind his own loft, it had been messy and risky, but Carle got away clean. The second one, however, Carle brought a custom-made billy club that fit in a holster in his lower back. It was eleven inches long and weighted at the business end. Boys two-through-six were ended in various locations and found soon after by authorities. The papers began seeking information on "The Reaper" and Carle enjoyed his new moniker.

Carle checked his watch, it was three-thirty, time to head home. His apartment was on site, but at the far end, two kilometers away. He would walk, the evening cool and dry. As he turned for the sidewalk, passing the main ring and then the secondary dressage arena, he fell into his thoughts.

Ten… I guess I'll look for number eleven. I will have peace when I'm done. There is no doubt.

Ten minutes later and deep in thought, a person on a bicycle rode past and popped the back of his head with gusto.

"Dammt! zur Seite rücken!"[2] the young man said and moved on up the path. This sidewalk intersected the town park but rarely did a cyclist come so close to where he walked.

It may have ended there; a rude idiot slapping strangers as he passed. But before he was out of earshot, he laughed, high and shrill. Carle's skin prickled with purpose. He picked up his pace and broke into a jog, surreptitiously following the youngster's progress. The boy wouldn't notice the tail. Carle was an expert, trained by the top, the Elite, the best US Special Forces instructors money could buy. He'd hired Americans because the German government was too familiar with his family name. The four servicemen who trained him over the course of a year came and went, entirely hidden on the family estate. Carle's mother and brothers assumed he was training to enter the military himself, but no, the stealth, agility, and combat skills they taught him would serve to make him an excellent killer. And it had. This new laughing boy would not see him coming.

In less than ten minutes, the boy reached his domicile, a two-story townhouse attached to a row of six others. He steered his bike between two rows of

---

[2] "Move over, move aside!" (German)

homes and disappeared. Carle pulled behind a nearby bus station shelter to watch and wait. The timing meant the boy had returned home from school. He might be alone, Mom and Dad at work. Most of the middle-class boys Carle hunted had two working parents.

Carle needed to know, he needed to look inside. When the road showed no movement up or down, he jogged along the decorative trees to the home's outer wall. From there, he flattened against the stone and crept to the back. This had worked before and he grinned. The back door was of sliding glass and with a quick check to see the interior room clear, he checked the lock. It was open.

Meant to be! he said inside and crept into a small mudroom.

In two silent steps, Carle pushed a swinging door opening into a modern kitchen. From here, the sounds of laughter emitted from an upcoming room and Carle narrowed his eyes. That sound, that giggle, could have been one of the original six if they weren't certainly deceased. Carle moved without a sound to the next doorless threshold and peeked. The laughing boy had dropped himself into a sofa facing a 72" television, game-controller in hand. Carle stared at the back of his head. This boy wasn't Caucasian like the boys who killed his father, but he had the same laugh. Even now, pointing at the screen, arrogant shouts of his abilities and greatness, then giggling at something heard over the earphones, playing other people in the same online game. *Oh, this is good.* If Carle ended him with these other people listening, it may further assuage the pain in Carle's tortured spirit.

The youngster laughed again, kicking his legs into the air with abandon. *"Arschloch dummkopf!"*[3] he giggled, shaking his head at whatever his friends were saying.

Yes, this boy would have swung a bat at my dad's head. He

---

[3] (German curse word/slang)

would have done it. He doesn't have to be blond to be evil.

Carle slipped into the room unnoticed, the boy immersed in his video fun. He then barked a new huge laugh, flailing his body with gusto. Then he shouted in English, "You're such an idiot!" furiously wiggling the knobs of his controller.

Carle stood directly behind him and the boy remained clueless. Maybe he could let this one go. Maybe he was done killing. He pondered his choices as on the enormous screen, a CGI policeman approached a group of men standing around a barrel fire. Carle could plainly see his reflection as he stood behind the feckless youth who he now saw controlled the gun-wielding cop. Just then, the characters around the fire turned to see the cop; they were not criminals, but NPCs filling the background of the downtown's saddest area. The boy tuned his gun to them and fired, mouth noises matching the machine-gun rat-tat-tat his fake game gun echoed.

"Got 'em!" he called out in English, cackling in fun. That noise was all Carle needed to proceed, to initiate the cleansing that would erase another laughing boy from the planet.

His friends will hear...

Carle would wait until the moment the boy noticed him in the monitor's reflection. He'd make a move, catch the kid's eye, and zoom in, grasping his throat, allowing him to cry out for his gaming team, but not loud enough to alert the neighbors.

Then it happened; the boy's eyes turned to his reflection.

Exactly as planned, Carle had the boy's throat in his huge hands. The boy shouted in German, "*DER SCHNITTER!*"[4] and was silenced by the attack, his larynx crushed. Calls from the headset reached Carle's ears.

---

[4] The Reaper (German)

"Banner? Hey, what did you say?"
"He said *schnitter.*"
"The Reaper? You ass! That's not funny!"
"B! You're missing the target!"
"He's gonna screw this up again."
"Come back!"

Carle unplugged the headphones with an easy smile, the boy muted by Carle's left hand pressing closed his throat. He could barely breathe and his struggling had grown weaker. He couldn't have weighed more than ninety pounds, no challenge for Carle's size. Banner would never speak again. Carle yanked the boy's body over the back of the couch.

"Bitte! Bitte!" His mouth formed the words but only the hiss of air passed his lips.

Carle sent the boy a wink, reached behind him to his stick and pulled it free. When the boy saw the club, his eyes sprang tears. It didn't take much. Three sharp raps to the skull and the kid's lights went out. More than even before, peace surged through Carle's system, a happiness and sense of accomplishment that only arose when he ended one of these laughing boys. He would sleep well tonight! But first, he needed to get out. He would leave the corpse as it sat. The papers could add this to his profile. It was sort of making him famous and Carle grinned.

5 | The Other Woman

Lord, who may abide in Your tabernacle?
Who may dwell in Your holy hill?
He who walks uprightly,
And works righteousness,
Psalm 15:1-2

HOPE DIDN'T HURT FOR MONEY; upon his untimely death in an auto accident, her husband left behind a sizable insurance policy. Still, she expected Mark to will to her his German estate if his plan to be delivered of vampirism included him leaving the world. Last week, careful investigation revealed her former lover *(hah, I wish!)* had instead willed the house Hope had lived in several months before their breakup to a trust under the name Elizabeth Hawken.

Who the flip is that?

Hope's curiosity ran deep and she pondered the name a long time before she finally decided to dig into the internet for answers. There were too many Elizabeth Hawkenses to search alone, so she coupled the name with Mark's known associates. After an exhaustive search, she focused down on a California couple, Reverend Aaron and Mrs. Elizabeth Hawken. A little more digging revealed Mrs. Hawken had recently divorced, she was a sculptor, and she rented studio space in Montgomery, Alabama. A couple more overturned rocks spelled out that the woman's father was none other than Detective Jonah Miller of the Whitford City Police Department (retired), the same cop who questioned Hope harshly about her relationship with Mark and Paul a year ago.

Why did Mark leave her his holdings here?

Hope had to know. Two months ago when she used the vampire magician to test Mark's devotion, her vampire companion failed miserably. When he then asked her to join him in the USA, she refused. When the feckless Androni the Magnificent kissed her and then took her blood, Hope realized all of the time she spent with Mark had been a waste. He could have taken their relationship further as she desired, but he chose to play the stoic loner-vampire card. *I can't have sex, I can't get married, I am not a man, blah-blah-blah.*

In his romantic though meaningless way, Androni proved Mark to be a liar, which was the catalyst Hope needed to move on.

And Androni? He loved himself and himself alone. The vampire magician had flown to the States at Mark's command and Hope hadn't seen him since.

But back to the original question…

Who is Elizabeth Hawken?

Maybe it was time to check in with Anthony. Hope opened a video-chat app on her cell and once she'd licked her lips and straightened her bangs, she punched in his digits. It pinged her old friend's social media and, whatever his faults, he picked right up.

"Hope? Is that you? Oh my God! How are you?" Anthony Agricola exclaimed, looking into the phone screen so his gaze was off center. Hope beamed him a smile, forcing nice and sweet *old-Hope* thoughts into her head. Not the *I-introduced-you-to-my-sexy-vampire-boyfriend-and-you-ruined-everything* thoughts that she lived with most of the time. It hadn't been Anthony's fault, not really, but if he'd never entered the picture, she and Mark (and Paul) would be off living large as vampires. At least, that's what she told herself whenever she pondered it too long.

"You look beautiful," he added after her small hello. "You must be okay. Thank God. We were worried about you when you wouldn't take Mark's calls."

A twinge of pain hit her friend's eye at the last phrase. He missed Mark a lot, which Hope heard in his voice as well.

"Thanks, you look good. Marriage is treating you well, I see." Hope's reply was trite, but he did look nice. He had always seemed nerdy before, but now he looked older, stronger, more confident and maybe even taller. She huffed a laugh inside, but wouldn't be surprised. Her old pal had been a vampire for nearly a year—that could make some changes in a guy. Who knows? She added, "I got your letter. Thanks."

Anthony nodded with a tight smile. "Are you in town? Sarah and I would love to see you. We have plenty of room. You could stay here." He shot a peek to the lens, so for a split-second, Hope met his eye. "We're in Paul's Montgomery house. The one Mark signed over. We're staying, we like it." He made excuses because he lived in a house that used to belong to the man who turned him into a vampire. And according to the news clippings of the night the awful Rakha Tep died, that horror occurred in that very same abode. Hope gave him a slow nod; she didn't require explanations. It was a gorgeous estate; she would keep it too if in their position.

"Speaking of houses," she said, maintaining her grin to keep it light, "who is Elizabeth Hawken? Mark's attorney contacted me about his estate, and he left her a lot of property."

Anthony nodded, his focus back to the screen, so presumably, Hope's face. "But he left you some, too, right? Four thousand acres if I read it right."

"Well, yeah, sure, but who's Elizabeth to him? I can see she's the detective's kid, but were they seeing each other?"

Her friend hemmed, blinked, and shrugged. "They hit it off. He had less than two months to live, he knew it, and this woman wanted to make it fun for him, I guess."

Hope watched Tony choose his words. He was holding back the God-talk and Hope sighed. "Just say it. God sent her, right?" she asked with derision.

"I think so," Tony responded. "So, will you come visit? I'd love for you to meet Sarah." Then his eyes widened with a memory. "Mark had two horses. They're in the barn. Do you want them?"

Hope's grin went to the side aware that Mark used the horses for blood, specifically to avoid drinking from people. She shook her head. "Nah, turn them out to pasture. They'll be fine. They've earned it."

This time Anthony huffed a sad laugh. "I guess you're right."

"Anthony, what about Androni?" she asked then. "You didn't say in your letter what he did when Mark died. Is he with you?"

"No, Androni went back home." Her friend ended his explanation abruptly and Hope caught on.

"What? He went back home, what?" she pressed, watching his face.

"Nothing, we're not in touch with him. That's all I know."

Hope narrowed her eyes; Anthony was holding back huge chunks of information. "Are you going to tell me what happened when Androni came there? Why the secrets? Haven't I earned the right to know what happened?"

Tony gave an exaggerated sigh. "It's not personal, Hope, it's just not something I need to be talking about. It's, it's…" he faded out and Hope heard what he wouldn't say. *It's none of your business.* She frowned.

"Okay, I see how it is," she said and dropped the smile that had been paining her cheeks. "Thanks for nothing and have a good life." Hope disconnected the call, a new anger in her chest.

Mark dated this woman his last few weeks. Androni left and Tony won't say how or why…

Hope looked at the clock. It was nearing three and she was two hours away from Androni's old stomping grounds. If his company was still there, maybe he'd gone back. Without further thought, she punched up Anna's number.

"Want to go to see *magie*? Androni the Magnificent is back!"

Her friend replied with seven thumbs-up and hearts emojis and Hope headed for the shower. Androni might give her answers. Hell, she'd give him her blood. He was safe. It was a fair trade — blood for info. With a smile, she worked up her beauty for the vampire magician.

6 | The Bossy Blonde American

Pride goes before destruction,
And a haughty spirit before a fall.
Proverbs 16:18

FINDING THE MAGICIAN HADN'T BEEN difficult. Hope used his stage name and discovered he had returned to his regular company. The fuzzy amateur photo online of the carnival signage revealed he had changed the name of his exhibit to "The Ghost and the Gypsy," written in German on the canvas, but English subtitled the website. Hope's curiosity increased, and as Ana, sitting beside her on the train, babbled giddy as a child on Christmas eve, Hope prepared to see the vampire.

I'll ask him about that woman...

Who the hell was Elizabeth Hawken to Mark? The train rumbled at top speed across the German landscape and Hope checked the cell service on her phone. Full bars.

"*Good, geesh,*" she hissed under her breath and opened her social media app. Typing in the woman's name, she discovered an unrestricted page, full access to anyone who came by.

Is she stupid or something?

At least her *laissez-faire* attitude regarding privacy meant Hope (and any stranger) could snoop with ease. She clicked the woman's photo album and her throat closed at the first image. Of all the insults! To post a photo of a proud four centuries' old vampire, hugged up to a mewling sappy church girl! Hope's face grew hot, growing livid at the entire debacle. The "comment" box begged her to reply and Hope's finger hovered over the button.

Oh, I could sure say something all right!

It was all she could do to *not* reply with a nasty comment. Incredulous, Hope shook her head. Mark would *never* have allowed her to take his photograph, much less post it on the World Wide Web. Add to that, Mark never posed with her in such a way, loving, attentive, sweet; Mark, tall, so sexy, and *devastatingly* handsome, towering over the petite brunette, leaning against her, his left arm draped across her back, that hand cupping her outer shoulder. His right hand held the camera out for a selfie.

His face!

Hope hissed, turning her eye to the rushing landscape outside the train. He had looked directly into the lens, mooning, fawning, and publicly adoring the woman like a love-struck schoolboy.

Where the hell was that Mark when he was with me? He owed me! I did everything for him! He would never have found God if it wasn't for me!

Hope wanted to clear her mind, but her anger would not be quelled. Mark had been king of his world when they met, killing sinners for God (so he believed at the time). When Hope came along, he began to remember how he was turned into a vampire centuries ago. Hope whimpered, wishing she could roll it back. One ear listened to Ana share her excitement about seeing the magier and her other half pondered the question of the hour: what in the world got into her vampire lover?

Anthony Agricola.

Oh… And God.

Hope exhaled and returned her gaze out the window. A vampire kills two hundred thousand people over three centuries, spends a few days with Anthony, and decides to give it all up for God.

Hope shook her head. None of that explained the other woman. How could he fall for a stranger when Hope was the one who helped him find himself? Who risked her life for him to gain his goal? Who was Elizabeth Hawken besides the cop's daughter? Hope would find out.

I held Mark's hand in his worst times!

Ana bumped her arm. "Ees almost there!" she exclaimed, her eyes to the landscape and the approaching town.

Hope nodded, but her mind roiled on the girl. A second photo scrolled in and it was even worse than the first. Hope gawked; this one had three hundred freaking comments and 455 "likes"! Who was Hawken? Some sort of superstar?

Hope studied the photo and cursed. In this one, Mark still held the phone, but he had swooped low to smooch the woman's cheek. Hawken's face laughed with such obvious joy. Joy that should have been Hope's.

That jackass! THIS IS MY KISS! she fumed inside.

"Oo! Who is that? Is that, er, *schwester?*" Ana asked looking over her arm to the photos.

Hope shook her head and pressed her lips together. Ana was the only riding student that meshed with Hope's personality, and Ana's horse was the same caliber as Hope's, a Trakehner with immaculate bloodlines who could jump the moon.

Thinking of this brought to mind their Olympic coach, Herr Gregor. The toadish man was forward and handsy, but she could deal with him. When Mark was there, the man behaved, but since the news was out that her paramour had died, Gregor came on stronger than ever. He wanted Hope in his bed. Not exclusively, but as a mare in his stable. Hope had only slept with one man, her deceased husband, Kevin. She would avoid

Gregor but would remain on his good side. He chose the riders for the show team. Position on the team was not based on performance, but on his preference.

The train arrived and they watched the station grow larger as they slowed to a jittery stop. Ana pulled her to the platform and then directly to the sidewalk. In two blocks, they'd reach the carnival fairgrounds.

Ana didn't know that Hope had come to Androni's show few months back five nights in a row. And Hope hadn't known the man was a vampire until he seduced her in his caravan, kissing her more passionately than she had been kissed since her husband passed. And then he took her blood —

God, I wanted Mark to do that. Why wouldn't he do it?

Hope recalled how gentle the magician had been. Would he allow her to come backstage tonight? If he did, would he kiss her? Bite her? Hope shivered with an unknown emotion and after fluffing her long blonde tresses, she trailed her friend to the magician's tent.

Androni's eyes landed on Mark's woman, his vampire eyesight picked her out in an instant. She had worn her hair down, thick and wavy, the color of winter wheat. And she knew of its power, using it to provoke any hot-blooded male within eyesight. It had worked on Androni just as well the night they met. Some nights later when he had her in his caravan, he touched that incredible mane, ran it through his fingers. Androni smiled at the memory. Why had she returned? Did she want another kiss?

Will she give me her blood?

Androni's gut hummed pleasantly at the thought, his tongue swelling in his mouth.

"What is that?" Joey sent his mind with a chuckle. *"Am I getting this fat tongue from your thoughts?"*

Androni stood behind the curtain preparing to go on stage and he swiveled to see the Ghost standing in the shadows, cheering him on, and now sharing Androni's longing for the woman's blood.

"Mark's woman is in the crowd," he sent with a warm wink.

"Ms. Hawken?" Joey returned and Androni said no.

"No, the other one. Maybe we will have her blood tonight. She is very enamored with vampires."

"I didn't meet her," Joey replied.

The audience hooted then, weary of waiting for their favorite exhibit to begin. Androni's heart clenched and he sought the cause.

Ah, it is the crowd… they will see the Ghost. They will want him…

The audience would ogle Androni's treasure, and the thought soured his mood. Rather than allow his sudden unhappiness to grow, he decided to go on alone and dig into the reasons later.

"I do not want you on the stage tonight," he sent to the boy's mind. Watching it all from the wings, he enjoyed Joey's shy agreement. "Good boy," he whispered with a wink and turned with flourish to the tent flap, ready to enter the stage with his familiar drama.

Barely had he bowed to the shouting devotees when Mark's woman, Hope Brannen, waved at him. He gave her a nod as he began his act and performed the entire show imagining her blood running into his mouth, across his tongue, and down his throat. He sent Joey mental flashes of holding her soft body close, his hands molded to her back and waist. Maybe he would touch her in other more intimate places… Whatever he decided when the time came, his young friend was enjoying the transmissions, although they embarrassed him equally. By the time Androni performed the final trick, he instructed Joey to invite the woman to the caravan.

"I will wait for you there. Bring her and we shall see what

she will offer us," he sent Joey's mind as he bowed goodbye to the audience. Then he scooted to the caravan to wait, the memory of Hope Brannen's delightful aroma filling his mind.

Joey didn't know what to think about the woman's brashness. She had entered the backstage area as if she owned the place and only when physically blocked by Eli, did she slow down. She pointed a painted fingernail down the narrow trail behind him that led to the performer's quarters.

"Look, fella, I am a friend of the magician's. He wants to see me. Just ask him!" she was saying to Androni's roustabout who delivered a lazy eye and a slow shake of his head. Joey stepped to their circle and touched the man's arm.

"It's okay. Androni will see her," he told the man who nodded without delay and backed up. Joey met the woman's eye. His friend was right—she was stunning. Slender, feminine, classically beautiful, to Joey she seemed a fragile and rare porcelain doll with a flawless complexion and enormous blue eyes. He had no problem believing she had turned Doctor Corescu's head. Any man – or vampire – would find her hard to resist.

"Hey, there," she said in a sweet voice, her brow arching the longer they held the gaze.

She knows I'm a vampire...

Joey had intuited the fact and wondered at this previously unknown power. He would ask Androni about it later. For now, he must get her inside.

"You're here to take me to Androni?"

Joey offered his elbow. "Yes, ma'am, this way."

"Thank you. Aren't you cute," she said watching his profile as they began the walk to the caravan. "What's your name?"

"I'm the Ghost," he replied, facing forward. She didn't appear to know his story and he kept his words few.

"How long have you known Androni?"

"...*He's just a baby... Where did he come from? He's American, that much I can tell. Did Mark know him? ...*"

Joey tightened his jaw, disguising the fact that the woman's thoughts streamed to his mind as if she spoke aloud. This was a new development and the first time he'd heard a non-vampire's thoughts. Swapping blood with Androni could have boosted this power, or maybe the simple fact that the doctor found telepathy so easy with her, Joey might have inherited that from him. Perhaps a little experiment was in order. Joey actively peeked inside her mind as he did Androni.

Hope's eyes flashed to his. "Oh, God! Is that you?!"

Joey offered a reflexive grin, not his own, but the one Androni taught him, the one for the stage. Would it carry weight? They had been practicing for his eventual addition to the show but had not yet tried it out on others. She appeared to receive it as desired. With fear touching her eyes, she dropped his elbow and walked the remainder of the path with folded arms. When they reached the caravan, Mrs. Brannen looked at the door and paused. Joey reached past her to push open the door and she shrunk back.

"You don't say much," she said without turning.

Emboldened by his success so far, Joey focused with as much concentration as he could muster and sent to her mind, "*I say enough.*"

Hope gasped, her hand flying to cover her eyes. "Please stop," she whispered with a tweak in her voice. "That hurts..."

Guilt tickled Joey's heart at her words but Androni's voice in his head requested he bring her inside. It was about to get interesting and he pushed open the door.

7 | The Stalker

My strength fails because of my iniquity,
And my bones waste away.
I am a reproach among all my enemies,
Psalm 31:10

THE BLONDE WOMAN DIDN'T INTEREST HIM, but that boy.... It had been an eventful afternoon that started with Carle watching the American and the German equestriennes boarding a train. It was the brunette he trailed. With his desire to end more laughing boys un-sated, he had been seeking his next target. This woman, Ana Berg, had three brothers. One of them was blond and naughty; he'd been caught spooking the pastured broodmares just to watch them bolt. He was around ten, which was young for Carle's purposes, but his laugh matched, pricking Carle in all the right places.

So, he watched the brunette today, thinking she might lead him to her home. When he sought her address, she claimed only a community post-box. He needed to find her domicile. He needed to end the next laughing boy at home. It had become part of his profile and the newspapers only encouraged him by their exciting detailed reporting.

And what of her other two brothers? Would they be home? Would they laugh?

Carle grinned at the notion of killing three at once. His middle told him he wasn't done. He knew with every fiber of his being that he must continue to cleanse the universe of these devils. The train had not taken them to the woman's residence, but Carle wouldn't waste the trip—the blonde attracted men everywhere she went.

Even at the Equestrian Center, they followed her like dogs on a squirrel. He smiled.

She may even attract a laughing boy.

Carle sat five rows behind, watching the backs of their heads. These women were self-absorbed spoiled and aging debutantes. Carle's lip curled in disgust. He didn't hate women in general, but loathed the *haughty*, male or female.

The train stopped, signs for the Karneval at Hapsburg plastered prominently for tourists and locals alike. Had they traveled solely for this attraction? Carle thought back to the last time he visited the carnival. It had been one across the border in Hungary. He had enjoyed the clowns and the tigers most. Now he was curious to see if the girls were headed there.

Carle watched the women disembark. If they turned right, they'd head into town. Not too surprising, they turned left toward the fairgrounds, where a short walk would bring them to the entrance gate visible from the station.

Carle grinned. The sun had set and the women made no notice of his tail. The blonde was already turning heads and Carle paid close attention, listening to his inner drive as well as using his ears and eyes. Maybe a laughing young man would appear. Carle could have a twelfth laughing boy in his grip by midnight.

Maybe tonight. Maybe tonight.

The women were so involved in their own conversations that they never looked back, left, or right. Carle mused that if anyone had designs to hurt them, they were easy marks.

Not my department, he thought with a grin. The two entered the fairgrounds and made the turn for the performance tents. When they paid their fee for the magician, Carle waited a few ticks and followed them in.

"The Ghost and the Gypsy," he whispered reading the banner over the tent flap. The regular magician at this Karneval was a man named Androni the Magnificent. Carle had never seen him perform, but his fame was wide. Unsure of whether this would be the same man with a new name, he settled in the back row, the blonde and the brunette several rows ahead.

Then it was showtime. The magician came out, he was young and swarthy, undoubtedly the Gypsy from the banner outside. He danced across the stage, his entire body fully involved with every hand trick. He flirted with the ladies and toward the end, invited one on stage to amaze the crowd with sight gags. Carle yawned, unimpressed. He waited for the bow, ready to leave. Maybe he could follow the American around the circus and choose among her adorers...

The portly local in the seat beside him nudged Carle in her clapping exuberance. The crowd loved the magier, it was crazy. Everything he did mesmerized them and more than once, the audience rose to their feet to be heard, as if battling to show the magician who loved him best.

The magician may have looked at the blonde once or twice, but it was difficult to tell from Carle's position. Finally, he was closing the show. With a few dramatic *adieus*, the magician disappeared, presumably out the back curtain, but the way he flapped his cape, he seemed to have vanished. Carle humphed and then realized he had not seen "the Ghost." Wasn't it a duo show? Where was the other guy? Carle realized he didn't care; the equestrians were getting to their feet and he needed to follow. By turning his back to them as they passed, the women stopped in the tent entrance and he overheard them speaking.

"Will you wait for me a few minutes? I'll meet you at the Food Court. I need to speak to the magier. I won't be long," the blonde said to her friend.

The one named Ana Berg said she'd wait, and Carl peeked over his shoulder to see the blonde bounce back toward the stage. She hopped upon the raised platform and ducked out the back.

She knows the magician?

Happy to be curious about something so interesting, Carle skirted the structure and spied on the blonde in the rear asking a cluster of roustabouts to allow her to pass. Their mass blocked a narrow path in the woods that must lead to the company's private residences. Glimpses of electric light were visible through the trees and Carle listened, hidden in the shadows.

"I would like to see Androni. I'm a friend," she told them in English. The working men said no, and a particularly rough one with a newsboy cap cocked sideways blocked her with his wide chest.

"No one passes, miss, move along."

But wait. Carle's skin twitched. It was a boy, approaching from the path, no more than eighteen, with smooth cheeks, pale skin and white-blond hair. Was this the Ghost? Carle watched breathless, his heart beginning to *hope, hope, hope,* this boy would laugh.

The young man touched the roustabout's sleeve, whispered, and the man stepped away. The debutant swooped in and wrapped herself around the boy's arm.

Oh, I need to know more about this boy!

Carle's body shivered with joy and he ducked into the woods. By sneaking through the forest, parallel to the duo, he followed them to a mint-colored caravan nestled in a small clearing.

Please, please, please, let this one laugh.

Carle hunkered down to watch.

"The Gypsy is hungry, my Ghost! Doesn't she smell wonderful!"

Inside, Joey snickered at Androni's telepathic message and he motioned for the woman to enter the caravan. After looking into the dark space a moment, she did. He took a deep inhale to determine if he detected anything special about her as Androni hinted. A flowery perfume, soap… Then he found it—beneath the obvious, an aroma that tickled his gut. He grinned when the woman noticed his scrutiny, flicking her eye his way before settling in place in the center of the floor. Joey licked his lips in that glance and this time, he didn't feel sorry for making her uncomfortable.

"Now you're thinking like a vampire," Androni sent with a friendly chuckle.

The woman turned a circle, unable to see her host in the shadows. After choosing his moment, Androni filtered into view by stepping into the weak light.

"Fraulein, how wonderful to see you again!" Androni said using surprise to his advantage.

"Oh, God!" she said her hands to her face. "Don't do that!"

"Pish-posh, you do not fear Androni," he chuckled ignoring her exclamation. "Please, sit."

The woman considered them on her left and right, hemming and channeling her to the sofa. When she took too long, he and Androni moved forward one step and Mrs. Brannen melted to the sofa, her eyes on Androni and growing wider.

She clutched her hands in her lap. "Stop trying to scare me," she said to Androni with false courage. She lifted her pointer finger to Joey. "And who is this boy? Did he come from Montgomery? Did Mark make him this way? Or Tony?"

"You will answer my questions first. Why are you here?" He lifted an eyebrow. "Are you offering Androni your blood? If so, I say, yes, thank you." He licked his lips and she blanched. Following his friend's leading, Joey joined him in taking another step into her space.

"Stay back," she said flustered. "Stop. I came to talk. I need help."

"Talk?" Androni said the word in a laugh and looked to Joey. "She wants to talk!"

He laughed again and sighed, leaning his long body to the wall and looking down upon her. She had to twist in her seat to see him and this put Joey on her blindside. Her respirations increased and Joey sensed her fear.

"What shall we discuss?" Androni asked in his sweetest voice. "I cannot imagine what we have in common now that your lover is no more."

She inhaled at the mention of the doctor. "I have a few questions about your time in Montgomery. If you could help me a little, I'll go on my way..."

Androni offered a tiny bow. "Proceed."

"Who is this boy?"

Androni *tsked*. "He is mine. The end. Move on."

Joey recognized the threat in his friend's voice and he enjoyed Androni's unabashed claim.

"Are you going to offer your blood? I am hungry." Androni asked, bringing a grin from Joey. He provoked her on purpose, finding her arrogance almost too unappealing to desire her blood.

Almost...

"No, I am *not*. I came here for help and you're being an ass." She rose to her feet, her head swiveling left and right to keep them in view.

"Me? Androni the Magnificent a donkey?" He sent Joey a quizzical look. "Did she call me a donkey? Help me out, Ghost, English is not my first language..."

Mrs. Brannen frowned and put her fists to her hips. "Who is Elizabeth Hawken? That's all I wanted to know. It's not hard to tell me. Why are you being so mean?"

Bored with the game, Androni moved closer. Joey matched his efforts on her opposite side and she inhaled, clutching her arms to herself as before.

"I told you to stay back. What are you doing?" she asked softer.

"Hush now, beautiful frau," he whispered coming close. "Allow me to see into your mind. Maybe then I will answer your question. You can trust Androni, no? I have been good to you."

Joey smirked as his friend hypnotized the woman with his words and compelling gaze.

"I only want…"

"What do you want?"

"I want to know why we can't be friends. Mark and I were friends." Her voice had turned dreamy and her eyelids heavy.

"I do not wish to be friends with you," Androni whispered.

"But I can help you."

"No," his friend said and flicked his chin in Joey's direction. "Do you see this fantastic Ghost behind you?"

Joey was only an arm's length away and when she noticed how close he had crept, even in her lightheaded state, she startled.

"Who is he?"

"This is my friend. He is the only friend I need. The only one I want." Androni tilted his head to one side holding her eye. "I do want your blood, though. Tell me you will allow it. Allow Androni to have just a taste…" His friend double-raised his eyebrows. *I'm getting that blood for us and I will share it with you.*

Joey's eyes widened. He would take it by force? So far, they hadn't done that. How would the woman react? What if she screamed?

Who cares? Think about it… her blood will run down your throat and you will come alive! Androni sent, stealing glimpses of Joey all the while deepening his hold on the woman's mind.

"Leave or stay," he whispered. "The window is closing…"

"I'm not leaving!" she retorted with muted effort.

She did not want to go, which Joey plainly read.

"*Enough foreplay...*" Androni sent to Joey's mind with a grin and his face disappeared into the woman's neck.

At the same time, Joey's gums shrank back and his fangs slid free. He ran his tongue against them, feeling odd and frightened at the sight before him. So far when Androni fed, Joey remained out of sight. But now?

The woman whimpered and clutched Androni's biceps but did not cry out or verbally complain.

"*Now! Here!*" Androni sent with urgency free of the woman's throat, his lips pressed together. His partner supported the woman's weight with one arm, the other hand's fingers pressed her puncture wounds.

Joey came in close reading that his friend wanted him to take the blood from his mouth... right over the woman's shoulder. It was brazen; and would she see? Did that matter? Erasing his thoughts, Joey moved in. Since Androni's hands were preoccupied, Joey grasped his friend's face and pressed his mouth tight. Androni used his tongue to push the hot fluid into Joey's mouth and he swallowed, his entire body alive and tingling. When the gift had fully crossed between them, Joey remained, morphing the contact into the romantic kisses his friend loved so well, tender and unending.

Androni maintained his supportive handling of the Brannen woman and followed Joey's lead, his happy sounds making Joey smile. When he pulled away, his friend sighed, staring deep into his eyes.

"That kiss was as beautiful as you, my Ghost," he whispered. "You fill me with joy every moment."

Joey remained face to face, the ridiculous woman falling asleep between them and he grinned. His body sung and his head had fuzzed. Could life get any better? He pondered another moment and his friend leaned in for more.

8 | The Trustworthy Servant

Deliver me from the hand of my enemies,
And from those who persecute me.
Make Your face shine upon Your servant;
Save me for Your mercies' sake.
Psalm 31:15

"THIS WOMAN IS UNBALANCED. PERHAPS EVEN mad," Androni said as he carried Hope Brannen to the lumpy bed. "She will need to be moved."

"How can you tell?" Joey asked.

"I discern an imbalance in her brain chemistry and a disordered pattern to her thoughts common in schizophrenics…"

"Whoa," Joey exhaled amazed again at his friend's incredible knowledge bank.

"I spent years feeding at hospitals and I recognize the symptoms. She should awaken away from here. If possible, in the presence of the young woman she arrived with."

"Eli," Joey said with a single nod.

"Yes. Please fetch him," Androni asked and Joey turned for the door. In five minutes, the man entered the small space, his eye immediately trained to the sleeping form on Androni's bed.

"This woman arrived with a friend and I would like to reunite them…" Androni paused with a grin, "away from this caravan. Can you accomplish this?"

Joey turned to Eli for his reply. Androni had only revealed the bare minimum regarding his long-time circus hand so Joey remained quiet. After a moment, Eli nodded, a movement encompassing his entire upper body.

"It is dark, no one will see me leave this section. Her *siostra*, er, sister, is waiting." He took a halting step for Mrs. Brannen's position. "I will say she fainted. I will suggest she eat more." He chuckled and caught both vampires' eyes. "She is skin and skeleton, eh?"

Joey grinned with a giggle. "Skin and skeleton, that's right."

"Ees right," the man repeated and completed his move for the woman. With care, he lifted her from the messy bed and carried her toward the door. "Very loved dee show, 'Droni, very loved."

He said his words directly to Androni and Joey opened the door when he was close. They watched him walk away into the night, carrying the woman in front of him. The air hummed the faraway sounds of cheers from the fairgrounds and closer up, crickets, owls and other creatures singing their nighttime songs.

After another long moment, Joey said with wonder, "And he has no idea you're not just another performer?"

Androni shot him a playful grin. "I do not know. He is a pleasant companion, but I know little about him."

Joey sighed in thought and his eyes fell upon Hope Brannen's purse on the couch. He strode over and picked it up. "I should run this to Eli." Androni agreed and Joey hit the door. With a little vampire speed, he reached the man before he'd made it halfway to the center courtyard where he assumed the woman's friend awaited.

"Eli, wait," Joey said low to avoid spooking the man.

"Yes, *pan*?" he said turning, using the Polish word for respect.

Joey placed the purse on the woman's middle and she didn't stir. He listened for her heart and it beat in a perfect rhythm. Eli noticed something about the way Joey paid attention and he raised his brow.

"'Droni like you much. This means Eli like you much, too. He smiles. Al *dużo*, er, all da time. You did that. You. *Pan* Ghost."

"I'm glad," Joey said in a soft voice, not wishing to rouse the woman in his arms.

"I have know-ed 'Droni seventeen years," the gruff roustabout added with a taut nod.

They stood side by side, so Joey turned his face to clarify. "That long?" he asked, thinking the guy must have noticed his boss did not age.

Eli nodded and removed his grimy cap to rub his head. "I was born in Warsaw, but 'Droni told me he came from Halasto, in Hungary, and so did my people. Eli is Hungarian. I feel kinship with our 'Droni. We are de same, he and I. Dis is why I want you be good to him. He is like family to me. Clear?"

Joey gave him a grin and probably because of his Dracula appeal, the enormous man's smile grew toothy and his already ruddy cheeks darkened. Joey turned away after a new thank you, and as was his nature, his mind was busily going over the man's every word.

Eli considers Androni like family.

Joey understood that Old World people were close to the earth and close to community, more so than his American friends. Also, Eli's total loyalty was evident in every word.

"You be good to him."

Joey pondered that one. Eli spoke as if he and Androni were a couple. A romantic couple. *A gay couple.* But what else would they think?

They can't believe we're real magicians or real Satanists as the read-up says...

Joey rolled the idea around all the way back to the trailer. Did he care if a bunch of strangers thought he was in a gay relationship with the magier? No. Then his eyes widened. Is that what Mrs. Brannen thought, too? She wasn't a stranger. Suddenly, he wished he'd thought of this before. What if she carried news back home that she saw the Ellerslie boy in a love-relationship with another man? Joey's deadened nerve endings tingled in a weird echo of what he felt in his old life.

Wait. Am I in a gay relationship?

He looked at the caravan door before grasping the handle.

We kiss. I like it. Is that gay?

He always considered Androni's affection as that— *affection.* And because he had no sensation below the belt, Joey did not attach a sexual connotation to any of it. It was how vampires behave, right?

It's not sexual.

So, it's not gay.

Above him in the caravan, Androni opened the door and his form filled the space. "What are you worrying over, Ghost? Words? Adjectives? Descriptive opinions of humans outside of this life we're creating for ourselves?"

Joey climbed the steps with a slow nod. "What matters is what we think, right?"

Androni closed the door behind him and remained by the exit, arms crossed, regarding his face when he turned. "Is this what you truly believe or are you saying what you think I want to hear? Be forthright, sweet Ghost. I do not play mind games."

Joey did not enjoy the energy the conversation created, and he rushed to set it right. Stepping close, he grasped his friend's upper arms and held his gaze, looking up until Androni lowered his chin. "I'm not playing mind games. Sometimes, my brain rambles on, but I'm getting better. You can see I'm more like you and less like the old Joseph, right?" Joey's questions faded at the end and he didn't know how to fix it.

Androni rolled in his bottom lip, seeming to be forming his next thought. He lifted a finger to trace Joey's jawline, ending with a thumb to his lips.

"I never gave a thought about what anyone thought before tonight. Let's forget about it. Let's go watch your circus." Joey ran both hands up Androni's muscular arms to encompass his throat in the same manner his friend did to him on occasion. "We could put on a show of our own. If people think we're a couple, they'll be distracted from the vampire truth. Makes sense, eh?"

A slow grin broke out across Androni's face and he nodded once. "Oh, my old regulars will be jealous," he teased in a whisper, his gaze moving about Joey's face. "Before I met Mark, nightly, my caravan sang with the rapturous music of my blood donors, each in love with Androni the Magnificent." His eyes flashed with humor. "Many of them believe I would never settle down."

"But you did," Joey said matching his expression. "You met Ghost while on Holiday in the States, brought him home, and now you're madly in love." Joey giggled his last words, but the logic of the yarn was sound.

Androni tilted his head listening to the music outside the trailer. "The Trapeze, yes, let us sit in on Polva and her brother. Both have been in this caravan to share their amour. You and I will show the circus Androni is nothing but a mortal man."

"Who loves the Ghost," Joey whispered.

Androni answered by lowering to cover Joey's mouth with his own and dove into a proper kiss, as deep as any he'd ever delivered. When he pulled back, Joey was laughing.

"I'm sorry, it's still funny when you go so long," he said and his friend grinned.

"Come," Androni announced and opened the door. Joey trailed him out and half-way to the fairgrounds, his friend tucked him under his wing. "The audiences will enjoy watching our love affair play out on the stage. I will develop a new show, one with magic and passion. Our new life will be fun and happy, and no one will ever suspect our secret nature."

Joey agreed with a nod. Androni pulled him tight and they entered the main tent where the circus proper would be performed. When they found a seat, the magician greeted those who recognized him and he grabbed Joey's thigh with drama. When several people noticed the movement, he leaned down to give Joey a light kiss. The audience watched the magician they loved woo the Ghost at his side. And the trapeze artists flew through the air with the greatest of ease. It was fun and Joey was no longer embarrassed.

"Raus hier! Du! Was machen Sie?[5] Get out!" a circus security official barked when he noticed Carle rising from his spying crouch.

Carle growled, and complied. He had intended to watch long enough to hear the pale boy laugh, but all he'd seen was the boy lead the American into the caravan and a few minutes later, the roustabout from earlier carried her away. Was she dead? Carle didn't care; he'd been busted. He bolted from the collection of resident caravans, cursing under his breath, he returned to the train station.

It's okay. It's good. I'll be back. I'll see that boy laugh.

Imagining the pale youth's throat in his hands nearly brought tears to Carle's eyes and he worked on his plan. And, oh, he couldn't wait to come back to the circus.

---

[5] "Scram, who are you?" (German)

9 | The Obsession

Have mercy upon me, O God,
According to Your lovingkindness;
According to the multitude of Your tender mercies,
Blot out my transgressions.
Wash me thoroughly from my iniquity,
And cleanse me from my sin.
Psalm 51:1-2

TONIGHT WAS THE NIGHT. Joey, a.k.a. the Ghost, would make his circus stage debut. The ringmaster had spent extra money on their new canvas sign; instead of the hand painted vinyl of the past, the new marquee read, *"Der Geist und der Zigeuner! Ultimative Magier!"*[6] screen printed and clean as could be.

Androni had been on the stage fifteen minutes and Joey's cue was coming soon. Joey stood behind the canvas partition in the backstage shadows filled with dread. Before his change, he had been shy. Even volunteering for the church auction where students were bid upon to do housework for the congregation had given him a near ulcer leading up to the event. Was he ready to do the magic tricks? Yes, he had practiced well and did not fear messing up. He simply did not like to stand before a bunch of people, and his friend always filled the house with standing-room-only crowds.

Androni had reached the last segment of the newest show and he turned to meet Joey's eye. The world stopped as it always did. Even four months later, since

---

[6] Basically, "The Ghost and the Gypsy, Magicians Extraordinaire!" (German)

they first met, his pal's surprise gaze turned him inside out.

"The creature I bring out for you tonight walks on two legs but is not mortal. He is not a man. He is a spirit…" his friend said in English while looking at Joey backstage. "For you to look upon him brings you grave danger. The Gypsy and the Ghost are a team, inseparable and immortal." His eyes now swept the audience who fell silent by the due to his eerie manner of speech. "If any of you attempt to remove the Ghost from my side, I will bring upon you the entire wealth of my fury." Androni spread his arms wide. "I will allow you to look, watch, enjoy the sight of him but that is all…"

Joey bristled with panic as Androni lit into Joey's build-up, how around the world, people wonder if he's a real magician, a real ghost, or perhaps a vampire from the Balkan wilds.

Joey gulped. *"Wait, I'm not ready…"* he sent thinking Androni might reconsider.

"Ladies, you behave," Androni instructed the young women collecting at the front. Each night, this group would leave their seats to stand at the platform, hoping the magician might use them in a trick or give them some attention. They cooed and tittered at his words and he raised his eyes once more to Joey in the dark.

Eli grunted and nudged Joey's arm. He held out a garment, opened it, and draped it across Joey's shoulders. It was wool, black, and lined with red satin. Joey considered his attire, dressed like Androni in a white smock and black leggings.

"Here he is, I give you… The Ghost!" he said with a shout and the handheld spotlight zoomed to Joey's position.

Forcing an attitude he'd practiced with Androni in the caravan, Joey lowered his chin, eyes up, and put his fists to his hips. Then he strolled onto the stage, scanning the audience left to right and left again, taking huge strides to stop beside Androni, both facing the crowd.

"Do you dare covet my possession?" Androni bellowed in his showman's voice, his gaze on the squealing younger ladies up front.

Joey peeked at them in his peripheral vision as his stage persona required him to maintain an aloof stare at nothing. The girls were indeed watching the Ghost and not the Gypsy. More than that, they were *wanting* him, *desiring* him, *fantasizing* about little Joseph Ellerslie of Montgomery, Alabama, in their arms and in their bed…

"AH! YOU'VE STOKED MY IRE!" Androni belted in German, breaking Joey from his thoughts. "Because you have looked upon my possession and wanted to remove him from me, I will allow you to see only one trick."

The crowd disagreed with vehemence, hooting and begging their star to reconsider. Androni played it up with amazing false indignation. If Joey didn't have to hold character, he would have smiled.

"Ghost!" Androni said turning to face Joey and so his profile was to the crowd. "Do it… NOW!"

Joey hit his cue and zoomed out the back curtain, passing Eli so fast that the man felt only the wind. The tent erupted with shouts of surprise because from their perspective, Ghost had vanished before their eyes.

Joey leaned against the storage box of the neighboring tent and listened as Androni closed out the show. In another three minutes, he heard a familiar step and he met the eyes of Eli heading near.

"Was good intro," he said in a nod. "Dey like Ghost berry much." He then considered Joey with a sideways tip of the chin. "You like him?" he asked and Joey wasn't sure what to say, or even quite what he meant by the question.

No matter, Androni stepped into view and grabbed

him into a warm hug, his cape billowing around them both with the drama of the movement.

"Yes, him like me!" Androni said against Joey's hair, then he lowered his face to Joey's ear. *"Him like me very much,"* he whispered and Eli had already shuffled away.

"Are you sure he doesn't know you're a vampire?" Joey sent to his friend's mind, sensing Eli's question was probably, are you like him, as in, different... supernatural...

"Meh," Androni sent back, now pressing his lips to Joey's cheek. *"He just knows I'm wonderful..."*

"You are," Joey said aloud and giggled when Androni moved to his mouth and nibbled his bottom lip. "Now you're a goldfish," he said around his friend's movements. Then he laughed more at the sound of his own efforts to speak with the impediment. When Androni had had enough, he backed to see Joey's face.

"I meant what I said in there," he whispered and turned them both for the caravan.

"Which part?"

"I am selfish for you. When you came on stage..." Androni cursed to the side and turned his gaze to the stars. "Those women were gobbling up my Ghost with their eyes. Did you see into their minds?"

"I think so. I think they were imagining me... well... having sex." Joey blushed but his friend's eyes turned hard.

"I didn't like that. Not at all."

"You're jealous," Joey said with a half-grin.

"I could say we will leave this place, find a life outside of the circus, choose a different path, but they will want you everywhere we go. Every town, every man and woman who sees what Androni has will want to possess you."

They had reached the trailer and Joey opened the door. His pal's voice was not hard, although the sentiment was not a happy one.

"What are you saying? It sounds like you're trying to decide something." Joey had been with him long enough to see the signs. Androni was talking it through and to Joey, this quandary had no solution. Anyway, was it a problem? He would never leave with any of them. He would never even *look* at them. Why did it bother Androni that Joey's vampire essence appealed to his audience? "Oh," he said with humor, "you're worried they might like Ghost more than Gypsy?"

Androni had entered and stood at the small kitchen counter. He spun to face Joey leaning back and shook his head. "You were right the first time—I am jealous. I haven't experienced this before and I do not like it. I also do not like other people to ogle you."

"You don't like it, and what?" Joey dragged it out guessing the end. He didn't like it so Joey shouldn't go on stage anymore. That was fine with him, but his mind extrapolated to other things Androni might not like. What if Joey did? His partner did not like to be unhappy and had always filled his life with things that brought him joy. If Joey did something he *didn't like,* would there be friction?

"Hah," Androni huffed aloud seeing into Joey's ponderings. "Maybe having you as my possession will bring me grief after all."

Joey's heart dropped to his stomach, for the first time hearing a negative connotation from his best friend's mouth. Androni held his gaze and although he knew what Joey was thinking, he did not apologize or take it back. Joey's heart constricted and he forced himself to calm.

It's okay, he's not dumping me... he's two centuries old... he's never had a companion... We can figure this out...

Androni followed these thoughts and still did not change expression. Joey wanted to know how Androni felt, but his friend had blocked his seeking mental fingers.

"So..." Joey choked out, beginning to panic and not knowing how to fix any of it. "Androni... what are you saying?"

"I don't know that there's anything to say," Androni replied. His eyes had darkened at the start of the conversation and even now remained in shadow.

"You told me once you didn't like fear on my face." Joey lifted a shaky finger to Androni's head, his voice choking. "I don't like that face."

"What does this face say?" his friend hissed.

"It says you hate me because you love me." Joey could barely speak, his fear of losing Androni grew second by second.

"How does that make sense?" Another hiss.

"I don't know. I just see it." Joey took one step toward him and stopped, afraid of being rejected.

"No," Androni said low, the timing of the word having a dual meaning since Joey nearly approached. "No, I think I hate *love.*"

Now it was Joey's turn to think. Had Androni never loved? Hadn't he loved his wife? Had they reached something that Joey knew more about than his friend? Love, friendship, human affection? Was Androni so removed from his human life that he could no longer understand that the most important part of love is selflessness? For the first time since they ran away together, Joey was prompted to *teach* his friend, and if he thought about it, he would recognize his knowledge of love came from the Bible.

But I haven't even opened a Bible since I left the States...

"What is all this? What do you want to teach Androni?"

Joey swallowed and took another step closer. He stood more than an arm's length away and he hoped his friend would close the distance. The pain of Androni's disgust was breaking Joey's heart.

"Curses," Androni whispered and stepped into him,

folding Joey into his arms and looking down into his face. The veil over his thoughts lifted and Joey felt immense relief. "Beautiful Ghost, what will you teach this old vampire? I will listen. I will learn."

Encouraged, Joey said, "I think I could teach you how to love. I'm a lot closer to my transformation date, a lot closer to my old life. If you've not loved in two centuries, it would be frightening. Is that the right word?"

Androni made no response.

"It would be discomforting..."

He got a little nod.

"Jealousy is sometimes experienced when you fear you might lose the person that you love." Being held in Androni's arms made all the difference and Joey's words came easier. "This emotion is rooted in insecurity." His friend's handsome face grew concerned.

"How do I become secure? I do not want this negative emotion. It is attached to my affection for you. I do *not* want anyone looking at you with lust, with desire. Who the hell would dare steal anything that belongs to Androni? It is preposterous!" His friend's voice grew stern but he did not leave the close proximity. He was truly listening, truly seeking an answer to his problem.

"You can't keep me in a box, though." No change, no response. Joey continued. "I belong to you, I want to be yours, I swear allegiance to you alone, but I have to have a life. I have to live..." He waited a few seconds for his words to sink in. "What fun is a Ghost you keep in a box?"

Androni finally exhaled and shook his head with sorrow. "So how do I fix it?

Joey sought his mind and then his heart. The answer would not go over well and he was reluctant to say it.

"You have to teach me, say what you will not say." Androni's strong arms still held him close, both palms gently running along his back, the man's hazel-green eyes shining with affection. "Say it."

Joey said very small, "I don't know how to fix it as a vampire. I would fix it by asking God to help. Do you want to ask God to help?"

Androni dropped the embrace but did not step back. "You want me to talk to God?"

The blood left Joey's face but he answered. "We could. We could ask Him. What could it hurt?"

"It could mean the end of everything. The end of me. The end of us." Androni backed away and leaned on the cabinet. "No, I will not communicate with your God."

"Because..."

"Because He took Mark away, and from what Mark told me, he took Paul away." Androni narrowed his eyes. "Aren't you afraid he'll take me away?"

Joey's heart seized; Androni was right. If he came to know God, he would not live. His flesh was two centuries old.

Androni whispered, "We won't speak to God. We will work on this together, without His help. I will learn how to share you with the world." Androni sought something from Joey then, but he didn't know what to say. "I will take your lessons on love, sans God."

Joey took a deep breath. "We could start by not putting Ghost on the stage anymore."

Androni laughed a beautiful sound, revealing the horrible moment had passed. "No, beloved Ghost, you are a star. The ringmaster caught me on the way out. He sees dollar signs in my Ghost. He wants to double our wages and he is desperate to keep us. He will pay us through the winter break to ensure we do not leave. The Ghost is in the show."

Joey nodded and took a deep breath. Working on Androni's jealousy would need to begin in earnest and he did not want another episode like tonight. The money would come in handy. They did not require much since they did not buy food, but they liked the freedom to travel. They kept Harry Bax's[7] contribution under Androni's mattress and had only spent Joey's money so far.

Androni stepped into him then and shoved him playfully backward. "We have a show in a few hours. Teach Androni how to do this selfless thing," he teased and shoved Joey again, causing him to sit atop the messy bedcover since the trailer was so tiny.

"Okay, first thing is we don't push the Ghost," he said matching his friend's humor.

"Or what?" Androni bantered back and moved so close that he stood between Joey's knees, still seated on the edge of the bed.

"Or I will be forced to thrash you," Joey returned in a silly accent and the game was on. With amazing speed, his friend leapt upon his lap and forced him to lay back. The goal was to see who pinned the other for the longest amount of time. So far, they had played a dozen times and Joey never won. Tonight, maybe he would surprise them both by ending up on top.

He brought up both legs, wrapped them about Androni's torso, called a loud "Hi-yah!" and gave it all he had.

Joey never did get Androni to the ground. Now it was moments before the next performance they would test what they'd spent the past few hours practicing. Through role play and laughter, Joey had schooled Androni on dealing with his emotions regarding how outsiders viewed his prize.

---

[7] Reminder, in ANATHEMA, when they left the country, the mystic Harry Bax gave Androni all of his money as a gift.

Once Androni made his famous stage entry of seemingly appearing from nowhere, he waited for the perfect moment to bring on the Ghost. Androni stole a peek into the shadows and grinned to the side. His favorite person had dressed to match with a flowing white smock, open to reveal his relatively hairless chest, tight black leggings and knee-high boots. He looked even more beautiful than ever and Androni prepared the crowd for his arrival. The rote sight gags and sleight of hand still garnered gasps of surprise and everything Androni did, the audience adored. Very soon, they would also adore his possession.

My possession…

Ghost was right. Androni needn't fear, his friend was going nowhere. Androni could see right into his mind, the boy completely trusting and open. Joey the Ghost, only wanted to spend every waking minute with Androni the Magnificent. The ridiculous emotions of jealousy and selfishness were a waste of energy. Satisfied, Androni reached the last trick of the set and began Joey's cue.

"This audience would never sin against the Gypsy, would they?" he asked in German. Joey had nearly perfected German in the past few weeks and he felt no need to translate. In unison, the people assured the magier they would behave. Androni stood centerstage and raised both arms up high, capturing them again with his powerful gaze. "Last night's crowd desired to take away my Ghost, my only friend, my beloved." He allowed his words to fall sensual, romantic, playing up the love story the audiences were gossiping about around the circus.

Backstage, Joey assured him he was ready.

"Prepare your hearts, ladies," he said with aplomb and ducked to the side to add, "and some of you gents…" He stood tall once more. "Here enters the Ghost! He flits from room to room and whenever I catch him, I make him pay for how long he makes me wait…"

The audience oooh-ed as a smoke grenade exploded at the back of the stage and when the air cleared, Joey stood in place, fists to his hips, a haughty and serious expression on his beautiful face. Chest out, he strode to Androni's side and they both faced the crowd. The dichotomy captivated them all: dark and light, black and white, the *ghost and the gypsy*. It was a wonderful thing.

"I refuse to be possessed by any man," Joey said in practiced German with a hint of his American accent. Androni gasped turning to face him with drama.

"Stop this nonsense! You are mine for eternity! What are you saying?!"

"I will choose my own companions! No one possesses the Ghost! I believe there is one in this room mightier than Gypsy—more deserving of the Ghost. More worthy of his magic, his love, his affection, and supernatural touch."

Androni sent Joey mental kudos; his innuendo came across quite believably, even though issued from a virgin's mouth. The audience cheered as dozens of people clamored that they were the one the Ghost sought.

On cue, Androni belted, "No!" and reached to grab Joey in a hug. His partner swished his cape and, as done in rehearsal, he used the motion to distract the crowd.

Joey zoomed out of sight only to reappear at the front tent flap. To the onlookers, the Ghost—true to his name—had disappeared into thin air. All eyes still gawked at Androni on the forward stage when, Joey called from behind them in a loud voice, "WHO WILL PROVE HIMSELF WORTHY OF THE GHOST?"

The crowd went wild, one hundred and fifteen souls twisted in their wooden folding chairs to see the Ghost, taunting them and impossibly on the other side of the huge tent.

"The audience will remain silent!" Androni commanded from the stage, holding his arms up, palm down, as if able to control them all. "Anyone who dare answer this challenge will answer to Gypsy's wrath!"

Joey had picked out a man, slight in stature, about his height and weight, but with deeply tanned skin and a straggly short beard. He looked no more than twenty-five and as his partner singled the guy out, Androni resumed his role, daring the man to challenge his magic.

"No! That simp? He is no match for the Gypsy! You waste my time, Ghost! Give up this ridiculous charade! Gypsy is the only one for you!"

"Ignore my former lover," Joey said to the man weaving his way from the others and taking hold of Joey's outstretched elbow. "You are the one to defeat Gypsy in the realm of magic, eh?" Joey spoke now in English.

"Magic? Herr Ghost, I don't…"

Joey put a finger to his mouth with a swish of drama. "I will help you. Shhh… trust me…"

The man's smile grew and he accompanied Ghost to the stage. They climbed the steps and faced Androni, all three of them in profile to the noisy crowd.

Androni's eye softened at the sight of his Ghost working the man, working the audience with skill and so believable. The shy and introverted Joseph Ellerslie would never recognize the powerful vampire Androni looked upon tonight.

"What is your name?" Joey asked the young man, his eye in Androni's.

"Peter," he whispered, looking between both men.

"Peter, say…" Joey lowered his voice so the onlookers wouldn't hear.

Peter took a deep breath and after a peek at his friends in the back, he said to Androni with closed eyes, "I challenge your magic for the affection of the Ghost!"

Androni stepped in to grab the man by the upper arms, not bruising, but weighty. "Look at me," he commanded in a soft voice and Peter opened his eyes. In a flash, Androni read the man's pain, his mind open and his heart wishing to believe—not only in magicians and magic, but in love and forever after. *"He is a romantic. We will drink his blood tonight!"* he sent to Joey's mind and said aloud to the young man, "It is impossible for you to steal what is mine, but since you want to try, attempt to lift that table."

Peter looked at the flimsy structure and it wobbled. Androni was able to move objects of considerable size, but not yet a man. He had hoped that with Joey by his side, he could develop such an ability that he might one day fly. For now, he toppled the table and pretended Peter's gaze performed the trick. He shot his eyes to Joey.

"You helped him! This man is no magier!"

Joey whispered again in Peter's ear who then said to the crowd, "Out-out lights!"

The tent fell into darkness. Women screamed and men shouted, and when the handheld spotlight lit up the stage, only Peter and Joey remained.

Androni had vanished to the backstage and he watched his partner finish the show. Joey would see what Androni saw in the man's gaze. This man had been ostracized and mistreated by family and friends for coming out as gay after yoking his wagon to a traveling activist group that raised awareness and organized protests. When the surge of energy expired, they moved on, leaving Peter and a few other locals now branded as "filthy sinners." Androni felt no compassion, but intuited his partner was nearly choked up by the sadness Peter held back.

"It is time, beautiful Ghost, bring him home," Androni sent and turned for the path leading to the caravan.

In the tent, Joey ended the show and the applause rocked the fairgrounds. In fifteen minutes or less, this man's blood would be running down Androni's throat and he was ready.

Once off the stage and exiting the rear of the tent, Joey looked to Peter who still hooked his arm in Joey's. "You did good up there," Joey said in his own voice. "Part of it wasn't show; Gypsy and I would like you to come over, have a drink. Would you like that?"

The man nodded and thanked Joey for the opportunity. Joey liked him, felt sad for the way the community had treated him and hoped spending a small amount of time with him and Gypsy would bolster his self-esteem. They wanted his blood, but they would also make him feel liked. Joey had garnered all of this from Androni and he gave Peter a new smile. Before they passed the last tent, though, the ringmaster barreled close, calling Joey by his stage name.

"Ghost! Thank you!" the man said in decent English. "Your newest performance has blown out the stops. Your audience is purchasing tickets right now for the final five showings! You and the Gypsy have changed my life!" The ringmaster, a chubby six-foot-nothing man with black hair and a ruddy face clapped Joey's shoulder. "Tell Gypsy—nay, tell Androni that because of you, my son will have the doctor he needs. He has suffered so long with his illness, but this new money will send him to the best!"

Without thinking, Joey responded, "Praise the Lord."

The Ringmaster inhaled and froze in place. "You believe in Jesus?"

Joey's blood ran cold and he turned for the path. "Have a nice evening," he called over his shoulder, shuffling Peter faster than the man could comfortably walk.

Yes, Joseph Ellerslie loved the Lord. *Yes,* Joseph shared the Gospel and claimed God as his Savior. But since he'd been in Europe, Joey hadn't done any of that. Would God be mad? Disappointed?

Yes, I believe in Jesus, but why did I say that? I'm playing a part; I need to shut up. I'm sorry, Androni, I---

Joey's inner concerns morphed into a telepathic message to his friend who picked up and soothed him with his return reply.

"You did nothing wrong, my Ghost. Bring our friend. I will see how delicious he is for us both!"

Joey was happy he hadn't angered Androni and he made small talk with Peter until they reached the caravan. Once there, he entered and invited Peter inside. The young man climbed the steps and came to a halt in the center of the small space. Joey had wanted to talk the guy up, get to know him, compliment him, but his mind would not leave the topic of ignoring God. In his indecision, Androni took over, stepping from the dark corner to greet their guest.

"Peter! You should join our show. They loved you! And so handsome…" Androni stepped up and touched Peter's cheek.

Joey made sounds of agreement, but his mind pictured the round eyes of the surprised ringmaster.

"How does it feel, Peter, to have won the Gypsy and the Ghost? Will this make your friends jealous?" Androni asked, stroking his face and moving into position to take the man's blood.

Joey saw all this peripherally, inside wondering if he should repent. *I believe in Jesus… why am I moving so far away from Him?*

"You bet, Herr Gypsy, you bet!" Peter said with exuberance and then softened his voice to add, "They'll never believe it…"

"Would you allow me to kiss you," Androni asked and Joey heard the man accept. He was enamored and had a difficult time believing a man as gorgeous as Androni would be interested in him at all. But Joey was looking at his own hands.

Did I forget my first love?

Androni moved in for a kiss, his touch bringing up the man's respirations. He wasn't afraid, rather, only aroused and Androni worked him further by moving in for gentle kiss to the man's jaw. The swoon had begun.

Joseph stepped back and as Gypsy deepened the kiss, his stomach knotted at the thought of the blood Androni would soon take. He could take the man's blood…

I could. I would be alive. I would remember what it's like to have sensation in my toes and fingers, I would feel it all.

But he didn't. He listened to Androni's heart, and to that of their visitor, and soon heard moans that crossed the line between amour, fear, and pleasure.

Joey waited.

And when Androni was done, he would share.

But why won't I speak to God?

Joey wasn't sure, but he wouldn't. No way, no how.

10 | The Roustabout

Behold, I was brought forth in iniquity,
And in sin my mother conceived me.
Behold, You desire truth in the inward parts,
And in the hidden part You will make me to know wisdom.
Psalm 51:5-6

TONY HADN'T USED HIS PASSPORT SINCE 2010 when the church leaders attended a denominational conference in Nova Scotia, Canada. Now that he had arrived at Leipzig/Halle Airport, he found most of the signage translated into English and the ones that weren't were easily understood in context. Because of this, Tony found baggage claim and then the cabstand in short order.

Another huge help turned out to be that the Germans he spoke to understood him and most of them replied in his language. Tony only knew English, but recalled with a sad grin one of Mark's conversations about how easy it was to learn new skills as a vampire.

But I had enough on my hands simply avoiding drinking blood, Tony thought with a wry inner grin. Now to find the circus.

Because of Mark's input before his passing, Tony knew the general state the man's carnival occupied, but he would need to ask locals of its precise location. One thing that he found very helpful was that so far, everyone he asked had heard of the "Karnaval at Hapsburg," and they knew of Androni the Magnificent. Tony found the vampire's celebrity amazing; as much as he and Mark spent their vampire existences hiding from scrutiny, this "wild child" as Mark once called him, lived

79

it up in grand style.

Maybe it will be easy, Tony thought. *Maybe when I ask to have a chat, they will receive me, let me do my thing.*

He had important news for the duo. Whether or not he would be able to convince Joey to come home with him, they needed to know about the private investigator. With no phone or computer, the only way Tony could figure getting word to them would be in person. For the moment, he hoped the taxi driver he'd chosen knew exactly where to find the fairgrounds.

"Karneval? Ja, yes, of course," the cabbie said with a nod and swung away from Tony's hotel. "Ees a fifteen-minute drive, not too far. Relax yourself."

Tony thanked him and exhaled, wanting to do just that. He was racing Andy Kranchez and it was up to the Lord who would get to the boy first. Would Kranchez hurt Joey? Tony didn't think so, but the man might have seen something he couldn't stomach—if he saw the demon vampire in Rakha the night he shot him, he might be coming to get Joey and Androni for other reasons.

Mark said the guy might have seen him disappear...

Tony sighed. He missed Mark, which still amazed him now and then when he fell into his memories. Only a little over a year ago, the same man attacked him, bit his arm and drank his blood. It seemed strange now that time passed and they had become friends and soldiers for the Lord, side-by-side. And Mark's personality and attitude changed drastically his final few weeks. Tony and Sarah enjoyed the light in his face when he spoke with Jonah Miller's daughter, Elizabeth Hawken. They watched a man, not a vampire, fall in love. If the Lord had allowed it, Tony was certain those two would have lived a happy life together. But God brought Mark home and Tony had stood by him to the very end. To close the topic in his mind, Tony thanked God that he got to know the man in the first place. The Lord's ways could be bizarre and Tony would always try to listen even if His instructions seemed nuts.

"Halo, look, Karneval," the cabbie said, gesturing ahead with a hairy knuckle. Less than a mile away, Tony picked out brightly colored structures and scooted forward to speak to the man between the seats.

"Have you ever seen the magician's show? Androni the Magnificent?" he asked and the driver grumbled with a shake of his head.

"Everyone in the land has seen his show, but I warn you. Do not take a woman you love, for that scoundrel will steal her away, *verstehst du*? Do you understand? He took my girl and I never saw her again!"

Hope had gone to Androni's trailer last year and discovered he was a vampire. The driver read something in his face and added more.

"She is fine, no, I mean we are no more," he said with a sad nod. He was pulling them into a circular drive before the entry gate and he put the car into park.

Tony commiserated and thanked him for the ride, ready to explore the fairgrounds and find Joey and Androni. He faced the conglomeration of various tents and vendor booths, reading the garish hand-painted signs and fluttering banners. Further in, a kaleidoscope played a carousel tune and Tony headed through the unmanned entry gate. It was early, only food trucks and animal exhibits operating, evident by the limited number of patrons ambling in the early afternoon sunshine.

By using the facility map located on the City of Hapsburg's website, in another five minutes, he located the quiet and shuttered magician's tent. A man's movement around the side caught Tony's attention and he circumnavigated to the rear to find a husky character loading crates onto a trailer. With no one else in sight, Tony stepped up and greeted the man.

"Guten tag, Herr. Sprichst du Englisch?" he asked using the single most useful phrase he'd learned on the flight.

"Ja, yes, guten tag," he answered, barely looking up, engrossed in his task.

With no other laborers in sight, Tony rolled up his sleeves and pointed to the boxes on his side. "Can I help?" he asked.

The man looked left, right, and left again and met Tony's eye. "Dey sleep, Eli works! Yes, help. That is good!"

His humor brought a grin and Tony hefted the first box. It was empty so he assumed they were piling them onto the trailer to be returned. Up and down, forward and back, and fifty-five crates were loaded and tied down in twenty minutes. Eli checked his rope knots and turned to Tony with a new grin.

"You have cut my work in half!" The man removed his newsboy cap, wiped his brow with his pocket cloth, and returned it sideways on his head. "Thank you! Come, I will give you drink."

Tony thanked him and daubed his sweaty forehead with his sleeve. November in Germany was much like Alabama for the moment and he did not roll down his sleeves. He followed the man to a neighboring tent where he stopped at a refrigerated chest. He lobbed Tony a bottled water and opened one for himself. Tony drank, ready to begin asking about Androni. This man was fifty-ish and not German, maybe Polish or Russian—Tony was still trying to place his accent from the various movies and television shows he'd seen. The man's thick body appeared hard, as if reflecting a life of physical labor.

When he finished his drink, he dropped the plastic in a nearby bin and put out his hand. "I am Eli Rota, chief roustabout."

They shook hands and Tony said, "Tony Agricola, I'm happy to meet you."

"It is good, herr Agricola."

"Call me Tony," he said and the man grinned.

He tucked his cloth back into his pocket with a nod. "Tony, Tony, that is easy to say. I like that." Eli clapped his hands together. "You look North and South and see only Eli. They all sleep like dogs in de sun, but Eli works. Sometimes I start before de sun is even up!" he said with obvious pride.

Tony smiled with agreement. "I'm the same way, too early everywhere I go." Then he huffed. "Like here, today. I'm looking for one of the company members and it's hours before the exhibits begin." He shook his head smiling.

The roustabout's face brightened. "Eli knows everyone at the Karneval. Who do you wish to see? I will take you."

With inner joy, Tony praised God in his heart for sending him to someone willing to help. "I have come to see Androni and a friend of mine from back home, a young man named Joseph."

Eli's face read suspicion and his expression dropped. "Androni is in my care. He not see strangers."

Tony jumped in to fix the man's protective tone. "Oh, we're not strangers, I mean, I'm a preacher and the boy, Joey, is the son of another preacher who asked me to check on him while I'm here."

"Ah, church people," Eli said nodding his upper body. "Androni no visit chapel. Perhaps you only need to see the boy and not Androni."

"If you gave Androni my message, I'm sure he'd want to see me. Besides checking on the young man, I need to update him on a mutual friend of ours back home." Tony was about to stretch the truth and he apologized to God in his heart. "If you would mention the name Mark, he will be grateful you connected us."

His plan was working. The man twisted his cap in his hands and narrowed his eyes, but he believed Tony and wanted to make his boss glad.

Then Tony closed with, "My plan is to speak to

them and head back to my hotel. My flight leaves tomorrow night, so I sure would appreciate your help, Eli."

Eli tipped his chin to Tony, a slow smile returning to his face. "I think you are good man. Androni will think so, too. And the boy? He is, how do you say? *Wunderbar,* wonderful. All here love him, all folk, young and old. He brings us a happy time."

Tony smiled and inside wondered how Joey garnered this reputation in such a short time. The show had been renamed, The Gypsy and the Ghost. Had he been on stage? Tony decided to ask.

"Oh, yes!" the man asserted. "The Ghost is a great magician. Powerful. And more important, he makes my Androni happy. In seventeen years, my *meister*[8] has never smiled as he does with the Ghost by his side." Eli sighed and looked into the sky. "Ja, the Gypsy loves the Ghost and the Ghost loves the Gypsy. This gives me great comfort."

Tony offered an agreeing sound, thinking of what he described. The performing vampires were pretending to be a couple. Interesting. Tony listened as the roustabout explained more about what Joey and Androni did in their act. Then the hour chimed on Tony's watch and the man closed his tale.

"I enjoyed our talk, Tony Agricola," Eli said and then added, "Agricola. You are Italian?"

Tony gave a little shrug. "The name certainly is, but the rest?" Tony had researched his family name as part of a church project but had not spent the money to go beyond the free peek.

Eli chuckled. "Do you believe Eli is Hungarian?" He nodded at Tony's puzzled expression. "Yes, when I tell Americans especially, they are truly surprised. But our countries border each other, tis' not too odd." Eli pointed to the West. "Eli Rota was born in Warsaw, but

---

[8] Master, Boss, Employer (German)

my mother, grandmother, and great-great grandmother were all born in Halasto, same as Androni the Magnificent. It gives me great pride to know our people shared the same land, the same water, maybe even the same blood."

Tony agreed with a nod wondering if the guy could possibly be related to a man who turned into a vampire two hundred and fifty years ago.

"Herr Agricola, I will see Androni at 7 PM. I will give him your message and come find you myself if he consents. Until then..." Eli reached into his back pocket an removed a piece of scrap receipt paper. On the blank side he scratched a few symbols with a quickly produced pencil and handed it to Tony. "You show this to any of the exhibits and you will have free entry for the entire day."

"Thank you, Eli. That is very thoughtful."

"The Ghost and the Gypsy go on at nine, only one performance tonight. It is sold out but this note will allow you to stand against the wall."

Tony thanked him again for the help and for the free pass and they went their separate ways. Walking toward the animal pens, Tony decided the first order of business was to get quiet and pray. Then he would call home. If Kranchez had arrived in Germany, he might update Bob Ellerslie. If he did, Sarah would hear from JoAnn.

Tony scanned the area.

Is he here already?

Tony liked the man but his agenda did not run congruent with Tony's.

"Lord, allow me to bring Joey home safely, and protect Androni until he can know you as God and King."

Tony whispered a few more requests to the Lord; there was no sin in hoping the night went easy.

11 | The Argument

Create in me a clean heart, O God,
And renew a steadfast spirit within me.
Do not cast me away from Your presence,
And do not take Your Holy Spirit from me.
Psalm 51:10-11

"WHAT DO YOU WANT ME TO DO?" Joey asked, exasperated. "Just say it. I'll do whatever you want."

Androni only shook his head, his eyes to the side. Joseph watched his profile, Androni deep in thought and blocking whatever had him undone. Joey waited. In minutes, Pastor Tony Agricola would knock on the caravan door. He had tracked them down and said he had a dire warning. The message he asked Eli to deliver laid it out; Tony wanted to speak to Joey. The second part sounded like a secret code: *Mark has a message*. Since the doctor was dead, Joey assumed it was to throw off Eli but attract a vampire's attention.

"Androni… please say something," Joey whispered. He didn't come close. Not yet. His favorite person's body language read loud and clear. For the moment, they stood at opposite ends of the caravan, Joey at the bed and Androni in the kitchen.

Finally, Androni said in a low growl, "If you loved Androni as you say, you would have nothing to do with this man, this *preacher*. He can visit me, tell me his secret, and move along. You do not need to be here. You know what he wants and you remain?"

Joey didn't have an answer fast enough.

"Why would you see him when his main desire is to

take you away from me?"

Joey parted his lips, still unable to answer before his friend spoke on.

"This pause causes me great concern. This proves you are not as committed to Androni as he is committed to you. This is unbalanced and I *do ...not ...like it!*" He hissed the last few words, his eyes sunken and nearly invisible from Joey's position.

"It's not like that." Joey stepped forward but did not draw close. "It's not about me and you. It's about God. Remember when you said you would have my mind and body and God would keep my spirit? That's all this is. It's about my relationship with God. I am still your beloved and I will stay." He had softened his voice but could see nothing of what Androni thought.

"You say that, but we're back to the same question. Tony wants to talk you into leaving. There is no question in his mind that you are wrong to stay with Androni. He believes—as did Mark—that you must reject Androni in order to be like them. A God-follower." Androni looked aside, still blocking his mental stream.

A few responses came to mind and Joey was afraid to speak. Ten feet away, Androni's face swiveled to his. His brow furrowed.

"Say the words, Joseph."

Androni's new tone hurt and Joey's body ached with dread. He would say it. He had to. In a whisper, he said without apology, "I have to have God or I will die." He licked his lips and said even lower, "My life is intricately connected with God's. We are one."

"What the hell are you talking about?" Androni said with an edge, the sound louder than they had spoken so far.

"Do you really want to know?" Joey asked without planning his words. He didn't like his own voice then; it was too much like his dad's. Joey slowed his breathing and fixed it to ask, "Will you listen? I want you to know this part of me. It's been hard keeping you two apart. But there's something about me I haven't shared."

"Keeping who apart? Me and your God?"

"Me and *the* God," Joey said and sought his eye. Maybe his friend was calming, maybe hearing. Androni dropped into the couch with a dramatic huff and flopped his fists to his thighs. It would have been comical had his expression not been so grim.

Joey approached the couch and when Androni gave a miniscule nod, he sat beside him, putting his palm to his friend's knee. Androni stared at his hand and waited for Joey to begin.

"When I was twelve, my family went on a hiking trip. I got separated and was lost. I called and called for them forever and when I finally snuggled my back to a huge rock to rest, God reminded me of the Bible verses I'd learned over the summer. Be anxious for nothing. Call upon me. I will rescue you. I am your present help. And those scriptures soothed me until I fell asleep.

"When I woke up, it was still dark and I prayed for help. I started reciting the Lord's Prayer[i] and before I reached the end, I heard my dad calling my name." Joey lowered his head, hoping the movement might cause Androni to look over, but it didn't. Joey continued. "I ran to the sound of his voice and was found. Later when we were walking back to the main trailhead, I thought about how God rescued me. I had not been alone. I hadn't been alone when I was looking for my parents. Jesus was there the whole time..."

Androni *humphed* but it was soft and harmless. Joey continued and gently squeezed his friend's thigh.

"Everyone proceeded as if nothing happened, but I was different. I had discovered that God is real, He's invisible, but right beside me all the time." Joey rolled in his lips. "He's here now. Has been here the entire time, I just ignored Him so I wouldn't have to face some things..."

"Such as?" Androni asked in a small voice looking down.

"Just what I said. He's here, but I would rather fill my days and nights with you. I didn't choose you over Him and He knows that, but I also can't talk to Him since we got here. I want Pastor Tony to help me speak to God. Once I figure out how to have you both, Tony can go. I'm not leaving you. Not ever. Not for anyone."

Androni raised his gaze in increments and covered Joey's hand with his own. "Go on."

"Pastor Tony can help me hear God again, but God won't make me leave. He doesn't do that. Do you believe me?"

"You told me before we left the States that vampirism is anathema to God's holiness. That vampires have nothing to do with God. That Mark taught you vampires are *unholy.*"

Androni had said the word with finger quotes reminding Joey that he had no religion and was unfamiliar with precepts Joey embraced in kindergarten.

"All that stuff in your head..." Androni rolled his eyes. "I cannot make sense of it, and that makes me unhappy."

Joey stopped speaking, remembering his partner's assertion that he had spent two hundred and fifty years never allowing stress or angst to disrupt his "zen." Enter Joseph Ellerslie and suddenly, his life is upended. Joey took a deep breath. Maybe they can talk about that. Focus on how to bring their lives back into balance even with Jesus in the mix.

"Yes, let's speak on your precious Jesus—isn't this what I am reading in your fevered thought stream?" Androni asked, an edge to his voice.

Joey cringed again remembering how much better it was when every glance from his friend was filled with wonder and joy. Did Androni even like him anymore?

"Curses!" his friend barked and hopped to his feet

in a blur, yanking Joey up by both shoulders. He looked him hard in the face. "Do NOT doubt me! I have done NOTHING to raise this suspicion!" he shouted close enough that spittle landed on Joey's cheek and chin. "If anything, YOU are trying to leave ME!" Then his friend exhaled, his eyes first in Joey's, then dancing left and right without moving his head. Then he swooped in, pressing his mouth to Joey's, his bodyweight following, tumping them backward to the couch, Androni on top. Joey kissed him back, his hands pinned beneath his torso because he'd been unprepared by the move.

When the lengthy demonstration ended, Androni pulled back only enough to look into Joey's eyes, bracing his hands to either side of his head.

"Tell the man to come. I will welcome him." Androni licked his lips and moaned low in his throat. "I predict your God will take you from me. But if I don't allow you to seek him, I will lose your affection."

Joey shook his head. "It's not like that. God doesn't do that. He loves us. He knows you and I are friends. It's not a given that He will break us up."

Then Joey saw in Androni's mind, *"He is so young. He cannot see what I see so plainly. Our time together has a limit."*

"That's not true, you gotta believe me." Joey mewled bringing up both hands to hold Androni's forearms. "And if it was…"

Androni remained close looking into his eyes and he raised his brow, wishing Joey would say it.

And he would.

"If it was, I'd stay with you anyway."

Androni smiled.

Thank God.

12 | The Visitor

Be my strong refuge,
To which I may resort continually;
You have given the commandment to save me,
For You are my rock and my fortress.
Psalm 71:3

GOD SEEMED TO ENJOY making Tony's life complicated. As he awaited his appointment with the vampire magician, he was spotted by none other than Hope Brannen. She made a big show of hugging and kissing him upon their reunion, but now an hour had passed, and Tony was due at Androni's caravan in minutes. Hope wanted to come along and she wouldn't take no for an answer. Her personality had changed drastically and Tony supposed that had to do with meeting and losing Mark the way she had. After begging her to leave him to it, she agreed to allow him fifteen minutes alone before she knocked on the caravan door.

He stood at the trailer, led there by the friendly roustabout, and sighed. Begging the Lord to help him do everything right, he knocked, two sharp raps. The metal door swung in and there he was, the teenaged vampire, Joseph Ellerslie. The youngster had always been pale, but the vampire's curse had deepened the effect, causing his eyes to appear larger and translucent gray instead of blue.

"Hey, Pastor Tony," the boy said low. "Come in."

This is where Tony would meet Androni the Magnificent, who Mark liked and referred to as a man with no guile. In fact, Mark had liked him on sight and brought him to America to meet the others.

The magician stepped into sight as if he had been purposefully hiding in the shadows. He did not resemble the man Mark Corescu described. Besides the costume and perfect facial symmetry, Androni's eyes were hard and his expression grim.

"Pastor Tony, meet Gypsy." Joey closed the caravan door as Tony was all the way inside. "And you should call me Ghost, okay?"

Tony looked at both men and nodded; right now, it didn't seem important *what* he called the man so long as they let him speak.

Surrendering his tongue to the Lord, Tony began. "You look good, er, Ghost. Your mom and dad are worried about you." He shot a quick glance at the magician whose gaze was unreadable. "They think you've joined a cult, and me, Mark and Androni—I mean, Gypsy, are part of it." Tony noted both men remaining mum so he added the part they couldn't know. "They hired a private investigator to find you and bring you back."

"They what?" the boy said in a whisper and shot his eye to Androni. Tony continued.

"Yes, and if you won't come home with me…" Tony met eyes with the magician. "I wanted you to watch out for this man." He looked back to Joey. "He was the one who shot and killed Rakha Tep. I don't know for sure, but he might be a danger. If he knows about vampires, I'm worried he might do something drastic."

"Androni," Joseph whispered to his friend dropping the code names. Tony didn't know what they were thinking so he continued.

"Take a look at this man's picture so you'll know him." Tony handed Joey his cell phone after bringing up the photo screenshotted from the MPD website. "I've met him a few times, but always on police business. He was fair and seemed like a good person, but now he has a mission." Tony ordered his next words and looked at Androni. "I honestly can't imagine him hurting Joseph, but he might not think twice about going after you to take Joey by force."

Joseph parted his lips but then deferred to Androni by looking his way and remaining silent.

"Thank you for that," the magician said finally dropping the aloof posture. "Have a seat." Tony sunk into the sofa where the man suggested as Joey handed his partner the cell with the picture pulled up. Joey sat on the opposite end of the couch an Androni pulled up a stool to sit in a triangle formation.

Androni leaned forward, his elbows to his thighs. "Before you continue, hear from me the bottom line," the vampire said. "I will not permit you to take Ghost away. But I want to know more about this danger. Please, continue."

"Good, okay," Tony said. "I know the rules. I'm not taking Ghost anywhere. Before we go on, I have to ask in plain language…" He turned his eyes to the boy. "Do you want to leave?"

"No! And don't ask me again!" Joey barked, his voice hyping at the end.

Tony apologized with his eyes. "Let me tell you what we're up against." He received his phone from the magician and dropped it into his pocket. "Andy Kranchez retired from the police department this year and is friends with retired detective Jonah Miller and his wife." He turned his eye to Androni to clarify. "Elizabeth Hawken's father." The vampire blinked to show he understood.

"Kranchez never filed a report on anything supernatural that he may have seen that night, but Mark believed he saw him vanish, and he definitely saw what Rakha looked like when he went into attack mode. He retired soon after that night, so I want to think he found the episode traumatic.

"Joey, er, Ghost, your parents first hired a P.I. out of Birmingham, but when the trail led out of the country, the case was handed over to Kranchez." Tony considered both men to add, "Why him? It must be God's idea—to send someone who knows us into the fray."

He paused again and both men reflected no opinion, sitting mute and expressionless. Tony gave his last piece of info Sarah shared minutes ago before he arrived at the caravan.

"This morning, Andy Kranchez reported to your parents that he had arrived in Germany."

Joey sat up. "He's here? Now? Could he be at the carnival?"

Androni lifted his palm in a calm down gesture.

Tony checked his phone for the time. "He could be. He has the same information I have. I was fortunate to meet Eli who brought me to you. Kranchez will seek you out, probably from hiding when he gets here." Tony returned a sorrowful gaze to the boy. "I was praying God would let me find you first. It would be smart to leave here right away and allow me to escort you. That way if we see him while we're finding a good hiding place, I'll be a human face to guard you. You're gonna need a witness if you run into him. He knows killing a man is murder but if he believes you're a real vampire… If he's even a *little* unhinged by his experience fighting Rakha, he will not worry about killing you." Tony finished with something Jonah confided in their most recent discussion on the topic. "Kranchez shot Tep between the eyes execution style after he was down.

That's not police procedure. I think it is something to keep in mind."

Androni rose to his feet and Joey followed suit. Tony stood a second later.

"Do you have a car?" the vampire asked in a smooth voice.

There was a knock at the door before he replied.

"Time's up!" Hope's voice.

Androni's his eyes went to the ceiling and he said in a whisper, "I had hoped she was passing by."

The exasperation in his voice brought a grin that Tony didn't hide. "I came in a cab, but Hope has a car," Tony assured and said with careful levity since he did not know the man yet, "with Hope along, that makes two humans to protect you from a possible vampire hunter."

Androni looked at Joseph who then turned for the door.

"Hey! What's the plan?" she asked poking in her face before ascending the steps. "We leaving? We gotta go, right?" She stood in the doorway moving her gaze from man to man. She'd worn snug blue jeans and a form-fitting scooped neck long sleeve T-shirt. Despite it being a rainy pre-winter evening, she dressed to be seen. "Look, I'm not mad at you for what you did the other day. Are we going?" She huffed at the delay. "Come on. Let's go."

Tony looked to the vampires. "Hope's car is at the end of the path."

The magician grabbed two garments, tossed one to Joseph, and then in unison draped enormous black capes over their shoulders, the insides line with red. Androni gave Tony a pert nod.

"Um, don't you think you'll draw attention with those capes?" Hope asked following them out. No one responded but walked in a semi-line formation down the narrow forest path to the dirt road that would take them from the fairgrounds the back way.

Hope continued to ask questions that no one answered. Tony caught sight of Eli in the distance, chatting with another similarly-dressed worker. He acknowledged the eye-meet with a tip of his chin and returned to his conversation. Tony said to the magician, "I didn't say anything to your man Eli about this. I only said I was a friend of Joey's from the States…"

"Ghost," Joey whispered interjecting and fell quiet again.

Walking behind and to the right, the vampire answered, "Very good."

The car became visible through the trees and Tony scanned left and right. The sun was setting, and he was the only one scoping for Kranchez. Tony prayed for God to be his eyes and picked up the pace. Hope continued to ask questions.

"Aren't you missing your performance? Will you get into trouble? Will that make the circus people come looking for you? Wait, where are we going? Will you need any blood? What if only me and Tony are there? What are we going to do about that?"

They reached the rental without incident and out of respect (and maybe to honor the memory of Mark), he opened the rear driver's side door for the magician to drop in. He did so without remark and Joey went around the car to enter the other side. Tony sat behind the wheel and Hope huffed when no one got her door for her on the front-side passenger.

"Sorry," he told her as she slid into place frowning. "I'll get it next time."

"Yeah, yeah, yeah," she responded and fluffed her hair.

Once Tony had them on the paved road toward the city limits, Hope started up her questions once more. Tony stopped her at, "where will we go?"

"I have a list of Mark's local properties and have been studying them for the best place to hole up. A place Kranchez won't find for a long time." With one eye on the road, Tony selected the proper file for Androni on his phone and handed it backward. The vampire received the device and Tony continued. "I'm thinking that once you're safe, we can plan the next move. Have you been to that town? Thale?" He waited for anything from the magician, who only shook his head. "Mark's estate is heavily wooded if the internet satellite photo is accurate. It's also his most neglected property, according the maintenance records I conjured up soon after he passed."

This time Androni nodded, as seen in the rearview mirror. *"Danke,"* the man said and handed back the phone.

Tony arched his brow as, in the reflection, Joey slid across the seat to sit against him. They spoke in whispers and Tony turned his eye to the road.

"How far is it?" Hope asked removing the phone from Tony's fingers. She scrolled the pages and Tony resisted a sigh. The file she examined was the one he had collected of all the Corescu holdings, so she'd see Elizabeth's there. Tony had labeled them EH, HB, TA and AM. He wondered which anacronym she'd ask about first.

"Who's AM?"

Tony rolled in his lips. He hadn't mentioned it, but Mark left two expansive properties to Androni. Hope figured it out before he answered.

"Androni the Magnificent!" she belted and swiveled in her seat to face the vampires. "He left you something in his will! Nice! I wonder what they're worth!"

Tony reached across to pat her shoulder. "Let's give them some quiet," he said as she re-settled in her own seat. "Tell me what you've been up to. How's the riding going? Didn't you get a new horse? Mark said you had a new one named Rusty."

Tony had said the magic words for Hope's expression morphed into that of a child receiving an ice cream cone. With her hands coming to her breastbone, she launched into describing everything about her mount, her lessons, her competitions, and plans for the future. Tony listened and nodded and commented and gave the vampires some peace. He knew they would need it for he'd been there. Sharp teeth and all.

13 | The Hideaway

O God, do not be far from me;
O my God, make haste to help me!
Psalm 71:12

CARLE WATCHED THE GROUP leave the caravan. The accountant-looking fellow who entered minutes before the American woman, led the way. Only the woman spoke, but Carle could not pick out her words across the distance. He studied the magician and the pale boy, walking side-by-side, now and then, Carle got the impression the taller man was hemming the boy or blocking him, protecting him. It could have been Carle's imagination, but he could not get a good look at the kid, hidden as he was on the away side of the magician.

But I want to see if he laughs!

The group moved away, and again Carle's eye ended on the magician, striding across the leafy path with catlike ease, the same smooth movement he used on stage. The full moon lit the area and Carle wondered what to do next. Should he follow them? Now there were four... But what if he followed and he saw that gorgeous boy laugh? Just then, the magician draped an arm across the boy's shoulders, his cape now eclipsing the Ghost from view.

Carle couldn't stand it. He *had* to follow. Using stealth and care, he slipped into the woods, watching where he put his feet, to track the group in a parallel fashion as they headed for what might be the gravel. The magician still clutched the boy against his body and may have been speaking to him over his head. Carle got a good look at the magician's face as they reached their vehicle. He looked different without the stage makeup, younger, more serious. And he was tall, standing a head over the blond boy and the accountant. Carle was 6'2" and the magician might be his height. The American woman huffed visibly when everyone entered the car before her. Carle licked his lips, entirely involved.

This was too interesting, this was special. For the first time in a long, long time, Carle found himself curious about something beyond revenge. Maybe this boy didn't have to laugh. He was plenty aroused already and he'd never seen a grimmer expression on one so young. Maybe his mission to honor his father was done. He'd know soon, because the four targets were about to drive away. Carle's Volvo was nearby and the road traveled three miles before it branched. He had time.

Carle stood from his hiding place. In the rear windshield of the car, the magician turned his face. Carle ducked. It was silly; no one could have seen him. Years of training assured him the glance had been coincidence.

Just to be sure, Carle remained low and crept to his car. Wherever they went he would follow. He had a new mission and learning more about and possibly getting his hands on the pale boy was his new goal. He would not fail. He never failed.

The boy will be mine! Then we'll see what I need to do to scratch this new itch!

Carle started his car and smiled.

Tony sneezed once and shook his head. The place hadn't been opened in years, maybe decades, judging by the dust on the surfaces of long-forgotten furniture and the cobwebs in the high rafters. On the drive over, he had not gotten anywhere with the boy. No matter how much he desired to mentor him, as the Lord instructed, Joey remained closed off. There had been a slight fracture in his staunch avoidance when Tony spoke of Androni's apparent obsessive jealousy, but he would need to wait for God to work it further open. All in all, as the four of them entered the musty grand entry of Mark's abandoned estate, Tony felt like a failure.

"Father, please, put Your words in my mouth. Don't let me say anything that's not of You," Tony prayed inside. He chose a direction and crossed the floor to the first open door. It had been a sitting room, couches lined three walls, chairs populated the center and bookshelves framed the floor-to-ceiling curtainless windows. They had no electricity, but Tony had grabbed two flashlights, one for each of the non-vampires, he thought with chagrin, and pointed his beam into the room.

"We could talk in here," Tony said walking into the room and then dusting off the closest couch with his hand. He turned his light to Joey's chest. "You said you had some questions for me about... you know."

"First things first," the magician said and pushed past Tony to take Joey by both shoulders. From Tony's perspective, he read only surprise and then joy in the boy's face as the vampire walked him backwards to a far couch in the shadows. Tony did not train his beam to their corner, but from the silhouettes Androni had set the boy down and straddled his lap to look into his face. The flamboyance seemed odd, but what could he do?

"I'll be back in a minute. I'll find Hope a good place to wait," he said but they did not answer. Tony turned and re-met Hope who was still unhappy about being ignored.

"What are they up to? They are acting so *strange,*" she said stressing the word and Tony offered her his elbow.

"Well, they are strange," he said trying a bit of humor. She allowed it and took his arm. "Let's go exploring. Sound good?"

Hope giggled and Tony led her away from the vampires. He would get her settled somewhere safe and clean (*enough*) and then see if Joey would give him a minute. He had come a very long way to just sit back and watch the vampires snuggle on Mark Corescu's old sofa.

"This is a cool place," Joey whispered to Androni as Pastor Tony left the room. "If the doctor left you some property in Europe, maybe we can fix it up, live there. Just *live*... like you said in the beginning." He watched the man's eyes for confirmation, and although Androni offered a grin, his gaze was sad.

He put a palm to Joey's cheek and held it there, straddling his lap and sitting on Joey's knees. "I wish we could."

"Why do you assume we can't? You're not afraid I'd leave with that Kranchez guy, right? He can't do anything to us. In fact, I think we should start looking for *him,* turn the tables, make him change his mind about messing with us."

Androni's smile widened and he placed a moist kiss to Joey's forehead. "You are so young. I said when I first met you that you might be *too young.* You said, *too young for what?*" He touched Joey's chin with his thumb. "This is what I meant. With only eighteen years' experience, you're not able to see all the facets your friend Androni sees clearly. This man Tony..." He hooked a thumb behind him toward the door, "...does not need to try to take you away. The investigator does not need to burst in here and threaten our lives. *Your God* will see this through. *He* will take you away and He will turn me to dust."

"Stop saying that! Don't you know it breaks my heart every time you say that stuff?" Joey squeezed Androni's biceps. "Try saying something positive. I heard a pastor once say we can speak things into existence," Joey said, although things he brought up from before his change were becoming more and more part of another life. "Let's say, Tony will say his piece and leave. We will find Kranchez before he finds us, and we'll convince him to go home. God will love me the way I am and let us be together. Why can't these things happen just as well as the doomsday stuff that you're talking about?"

"Because everything you just said, you don't believe is possible."

Joey shook his head but Androni was right. He knew he was speaking falsities, wishing for something that couldn't happen.

Androni gave him a kind nod. "See, now you are thinking like an adult."

The words stung and Joey furrowed his brow. "It's not childish to think that praying makes things happen... The Bible says it's true. If I prayed hard enough, God could let us stay together."

Androni sighed. "I haven't mentioned this before because I did not want to face the possibility, but I now realize it is a fact." He licked his lips and said in a whisper, "I have contracted the voice of your God from your blood."

Joey raised his brow. "What? What do you mean?"

"The first time you and I swapped blood, I found that I had more notions about religion, truth, the spirit inside of man, things I never gave thought to, even before my change. At the time, I attributed it to spending more time with someone so close to their humanity. But then we swapped blood again, and again, and again. Now, I feel like I can hear your God speaking and He is warning me our time is short."

"No, He wouldn't do that. How does that even make sense?" Joey asked small and not wanting an answer.

"From your own lips. You told me that God doesn't like vampires because we drink blood, and He put the life of a thing in the blood. I took your blood into my body and He's in it with you. I am hearing Him. You may as well face it, my beautiful Ghost."

Joey did not accept his logic and attempted to dislodge Androni from his lap. When he wasn't successful, he shoved his chest with both hands. "Get up! Get off! I'm not listening to this! You're wrong! Please, please..." Joey's heart was breaking and he watched Androni's handsome face, his gaze adoring as from the start.

Androni leaned down and touched their lips together, not with pressure, but light as a feather. He remained there, allowing their breath to intermingle and Joey worked to control his emotions. After a few seconds and his friend was still there, Joey brought both hands to Androni's cheeks and pulled them together. He dived into the kiss more than he ever had before.

"I will never let you go," he sent to his best friend's mind and probably to God, as well. *"I will die before I let you go."*

Neither of them said more and Joey allowed the kiss to dry his tears.

Tony stood in the doorway and watched Androni pull Joey from the sofa, speak in his ear, and kiss his forehead. Hope had been tucked into a semi-comfortable master bedroom where she found a chest full of knickknacks to wade through as she awaited Tony's call to assemble. She had no use for "God-talk" and that was all Tony had in store for the next few minutes. Androni left the room at a quiet shuffle and they both watched him go. Tony guessed he wasn't much for such topics either and when the door closed, he gave Joey a kind smile. "Let's sit down."

Joseph's eyes flit from the door, to the dark windows, and back to Tony's face, but would not meet his gaze.

Tony sat and continued as gently as possible. "What did Androni say? Is he okay?"

"He said I should get this over with," Joey remarked in a low voice and sank in a chair opposite Tony. "But he's listening. If you ask me to leave, end of visit."

Joey had spoken while looking at his lap and Tony made a sound of agreement. The desperation in the vampire's eyes was enough to convince Tony to honor the promise. Whatever Androni the Magnificent was like before he met Joseph Ellerslie, now he was obsessed, and maybe dangerously. Tony would not break his vow.

"Joey," he said and this time, the boy didn't make him call him Ghost. "Ask me a question. I will answer the best I can. And I will *not* ask you to leave Androni. As far as I'm concerned, if you will stay, you should. He needs you."

Joey exhaled and met Tony's eye. "I want to stay. I want to help him. I want to make him happy. I want to see him smile."

Tony nodded his support. "Those are good things."

"And what I wanted from you…" He paused and considered his question. "How do I let God know I still love him? Our communication is different now. I feel it." Joey offered a humble shrug. "When you were a vampire, did you feel separated?"

Tony nodded once.

"The doctor told me you figured it out. Can you help me with that? Can you help me speak to God?

"Yes, I think so. It starts with being honest." Tony

leaned forward over his lap. "Honest with your words, your heart, and your mind. Ready?" Joey did not reply, but Tony had to continue. "Sarah and I both feel this line of vampires is coming to a close. We think God is using you to bring Androni home."

"NO!" Joey leapt to his feet, crossed his arms, and turned away, looking all of ten years old.

"Joseph, you have to face facts..."

"These are not facts just because you say they are!" the boy spat in response, his tone carrying anguish as well as fury. Tony regretted his pain, but what could he do? God's truth was sometimes hard.

But it is also always good...

Tony decided to go with that and said the boy's name.

"Call me Ghost, dammit!" he barked still facing away.

"Ghost," Tony corrected, again not concerned about what he addressed the boy as. Using a fake name helped the boy separate himself from decisions he made. But this was no time for psychoanalysis; the vampire magician was waiting outside. How patient would he be? Not to mention there was a highly trained investigator searching for them right now. Tony sensed an urgency to close this part of the evening so they could move onto planning and he continued in his softest voice.

"You said that you love the Lord Jesus." The boy nodded once. "Then you are His disciple, correct?" The boy made a single nod and clutched himself tighter. "Is the Lord God good?"

"You know He is and you're wasting my time with these stupid questions!" Joey replied in a near whine.

"No, I'm going to help you speak to God. Is the Lord God good? Yes, He is. Can the Lord sin?" Joseph allowed one half shake to the right. "Does the Lord love you?" No movement but Tony continued. "Did Jesus Christ go to the cross for the sins of Joseph Ellerslie?"

"Yes," the boy whispered.

"Did He go to the cross for the sins of Androni?"

"Yes," he said just as low.

"Is it His will that he would hold you both close, from now until eternity?

"Yeah..."

"I can't say with 100% certainty that Androni will leave the flesh when he is brought home to the Father. But I can tell you that until you admit to yourself that Androni needs to accept the Lord Jesus before he passes away, your life is going to be difficult. If you choose to ignore God's will, you're choosing a harder road filled with disruption and dismay. When we work against God, our actions attract pain and suffering."

Joey exhaled slowly but remained facing away, unable to argue with what he knew was true.

"If you submit to God's will on the matter of Androni and Joey," he said and was glad the boy didn't shout at the use of his name, "it will go easier for you."

Joey's shoulder's slumped and he rocked back and forth.

"Resist the devil, submit to God..."

"I know the scripture, Pastor Tony," he said low.

"Okay, so which one are you doing right now? Submitting to God or resisting?"

Joey said nothing.

"Or are you submitting your will to the devil?" The boy flinched. "Think about it. Who wants Joseph Ellerslie to *not* tell Androni about Jesus?" Again, Joey said nothing, and Tony helped him out. "Right. And we understand; me, Sarah, and Mark when he was alive, we understand that you love Androni, and you want to be with him and make him happy. We understand that he brings happiness into your life. I see that."

"It's more than that," he said softly. "You don't know what it was like before..."

"But I do. When I was young, I was different. I

stood out. I was teased. Think about it, every single one of us is teased for something and to some extent when we're young. How we deal with it shapes our future. I want you to know that we understand what's going on with you, but in order for you to be able to speak to God as a vampire, you have to first submit your will to Him. I can help you with that. He sent me here to help you. I guess you figured that out."

Joey tipped his chin a single nod.

Tony had a sudden thought. Before God introduced him to vampires, Tony had been in the midst of rededicating his life to God, praying for God to open the eyes of his heart, as the song lyric went. He asked Joey, "Before the church auction, what had been your focus with God?"

"Umm," the boy hummed and slowly turned three-quarters to Tony, his arms still tight about his body. "I dunno…"

"Did you want to be in that church auction?" Tony asked helping him work into the topic. He said no. "Then why did you do it?"

He shrugged. "Well, Luke did it two years in a row and wanted a break. Abby and Scotty said that they could get some of the college girls to bid on me 'cause they said I was cute at the last Youth Supper…"

"What gave you the final nudge?"

Joey turned fully around and met Tony's eye in intermittent glances. "I guess I just felt like I should." He then sighed. "I thought that God was nudging me, like He had something fun or good for me picked out. I prayed that someone would choose me to do something fun and challenging that might change my life forever. Maybe it would change the track I was on. I didn't like my classes and I couldn't find a girlfriend…"

Tony grinned and waited for it to click. Joey looked up but he wasn't smiling.

"I thought He'd have me go into the military or pick a new career..." Joey lowered his arms and looked to the floor. "I asked God to use this auction to change my life. And..." He raised his face to Tony's. "I'd been going through a selfish phase, Abby was helping me, she said I should ask Him to use me to spread the Gospel..."

"I understand," Tony whispered, but the boy wasn't done.

"I asked God to use the auction to show me the next step." He sniffed. "I was turning eighteen and still a child. I wanted to fit in. I wanted someone to tell me I wasn't a freak..."

Tony commiserated with a noise and waited for Joey to meet his eye. He didn't have to say it aloud, everything he asked for came to pass. He participated in the church auction and was purchased by the awful Haman Troye who violently turned him into a vampire. Because God loves him, He destroyed that monster and put Joseph into the care of vampires that knew God. Now, tonight, he finds himself as one of the last two known vampires on the globe.

Tony began speaking his mind as if they had been walking the same mental tracks. "Androni doesn't know the Creator. He trusts you, he loves you, and you're the only person in the entire world, among billions of people, that Androni will hear."

"I can't be the only one... It's too much," Joey whispered.

"I'm not saying you're Androni's only shot, because God doesn't hinge salvation on a mortal's deeds, but He definitely set you in place to be a major part of saving the man's soul. You see that, don't you?"

Joey shook his head, but not as a no.

"You are God's choice to bring Androni into the Father's house. If you listen, you would hear God ask you what He asked me and John Jenkins in our own time of trouble. God asks, *who will go for Me*. What does your heart say?"

"*I will go for You,*" Joey said completing the scripture in a whisper.

"So that's why the Lord led you here, that you may be a positive influence on Androni Miklos, the man inside the vampire."

It was all true and Joey did not comment, nor had he any resistance to the points Tony made.

"Joseph," he said and leaned farther forward, still out of reach, but the illusion was there, "you won't have to *work*. It won't be *hard*. You only have to submit your will and God will do the rest. He will make it happen *through* you. Resistance only draws out the process. God requests that each of us would be part of the solution, not part of the problem."

"That's what I always wanted," Joseph responded. "All I ever wanted was to make God proud of me." He flashed a new gaze to Tony. "Before I met Androni, I never made anyone this happy..." He swallowed and added, "Androni loves me. He looks at me like I'm all he needs. When we look at each other, he feels peace to his very soul."

"Joseph," Tony said as his eyes swelled with emotion due to the meaning in his next phrase. He lowered his voice with seriousness. "Androni looks at you that way because in your face, he sees God."

Joseph Ellerslie could hold back no longer. With an enormous exhale, sobs erupted wracking his soul. Tony stepped close and patted his back.

"Let him cry let him cry, Father, and help him," Tony prayed in a soft voice. "May these tears cleanse his pain and give him peace. Stop the world and let him cry as long as it takes..." Tony fell still and waited. And Joseph cried for a long, long time.

14 | The Little Orphan Boy

Defend the poor and fatherless;
Do justice to the afflicted and needy.
Deliver the poor and needy;
Free them from the hand of the wicked.
Psalm 82:3-4

THE MAGICIAN, THE BOY, THE ACCOUNTANT, and the American woman had tucked themselves away in an abandoned estate house. What must have been a beautiful and enviable manor fifty years ago had fallen into ruin, melted by the sun, its edges nibbled by the encroaching forest. It was hidden in a secluded and lonely place, and as Carle tracked the vehicle to their destination, he estimated the property spanned dozens of hectares. Carle had found a great spot in an ancient tree to watch the north-facing windows, able to peer directly into those in the west wing of the crumbling mansion. The boy with the blond hair occupied this corner room and Carle watched through his binoculars.

So far, the young man hadn't smiled; he hadn't even laughed. This boy was serious, thoughtful, and worried. Whatever plagued him piqued Carle's curiosity anew and he lifted the night-vision binocs to see more.

The magician entered, gliding across the floor as if performing on stage. He playfully pushed the white-haired boy to the couch and fell onto his lap. The boy smiled, but didn't laugh. Carle twisted the tuner on his Nocs. The boy's face was a sight, smooth and handsome, his eyes nearly gray and emanating light in Carle's expensive field glasses. The two exchanged a word, and the smile widened.

What is their relationship? Are they lovers?

Carle left the idea open and watched on. He didn't go that way, but plenty of his contemporaries did. It had no effect on his interest in what steered the boy's angst. The two men spoke, emotion in every word. Carle detected zero evidence of lust or a precursor to lovemaking, so he watched on. The only thing truly odd about what he saw was how the magician chose to sit.

A new movement drew his attention and Carle swerved to the windows near the front double doors. The accountant was walking the woman somewhere, the two of them appearing to be in light conversation. Who was that guy? The woman he knew from the riding center, but this guy? He was American, his doughy, pampered appearance giving him away. He smiled a lot and even from the distance, Carle read the signs that this man was a counselor, constantly giving advice, evidenced by his head tilt, knitted brow, and hand gestures when in conversation. Carle returned his attention to the boy.

Was his mission over as he earlier surmised? If so, he could stop worrying overhearing this one laugh. Looking at him now, watching the magician kiss his mouth for what seemed like forever, Carle had a new and different urge touch his mind. He would begin pursuing his own interests, his own boys, and they only had to draw Carle with their quiet beauty to earn his attention. Would he need his bat? No, he'd use his hands. They were large enough to encircle this one's throat. He'd squeeze and watch the boy's eyes widen with surprise and then fear. Maybe the boy would let Carle kiss him. Would that be nice? He seemed to be enjoying it right now. The magician's face was still buried in the boy's and Carle touched his own lips. He'd have to wait and see what his inner self told him to do. First, he'd get his hands on the boy and then he'd know how to satisfy the void forming in his middle.

This boy will fill that hole, Carle had no doubt.

When the magician finally walked out and the accountant walked in, Carle watched on. And he pondered the smooth skin of the boy's face.

Androni left the room without drama, but inside, his heart raced. Everything the preacher said served to pull away his Ghost. He meant what he said, that a voice that was not his own was telling him to prepare his heart for the fall, but he refused to accept it. God wanted him to share the boy and God wanted Androni to die.

I just can't share him and I can't die… Androni's gut roiled. *I will not let this evening end without the Ghost and myself as one. Damn anyone who seeks to separate us!*

For a split second, Androni imagined life without him, the beautiful boy, now his other half, across the globe to never return. The panic that struck his spirit was so great that Androni shut down the images for fear of lashing out in anger.

I can't do it. I would rather be dead.

"But he told you that I love you…"

Androni came erect, every muscle on alert. What? Joey said that while at Mark's Montgomery home, saying *God loved Androni.* It seemed foolish and meaningless at the time and Androni did *not* want to hear it now.

"But he told you that I love you…"

Androni snarled. That voice was not his own. Who loves him?

Nobody loves Androni except the Ghost…

Androni sought his memories. Abandoned before he was weaned, Androni had been raised in a hospital-run foundry. The medical staff raised him and a few other foundlings to work. As soon as he could hold a broom, he swept the long hallways. When he could manage the mop and bucket, he washed floors. It was uncommon for doctors and nurses to assume the care of babes discovered in the littered streets, but in war-torn Halasto, Leipz Province, domestic factions vied for power over the corrupt government. State- and church-run orphanages were overrun with children left behind by dead, missing, or conscripted parents. As the internal civil wars raged on, Androni was sponsored and boarded by the local medical community.

Did they love him?

He did not receive embraces or kind words. Trained to be efficient, hard-working, and mute, even properly executed tasks were not acknowledged. Instead, if he performed the job, he received a meal. It was a trade that lasted until his fourteenth birthday when they put him out the gate and sent him away.

So... back to the question, Androni mused with a sad expression. *Who loved Androni?*

Melisha...

Despite the pain associated with that name, he allowed a tiny smile. As a boy, he had casual sexual contact with the other youngsters and later, with various nurses and doctors. Whatever it took, he thought, and he had no issue with sharing his body with those who provided his means. But Melisha was from a local family, the youngest daughter of a wealthy agricultural magnate, and at age twenty-three, Androni found work at her father's main farm.

Androni discovered in his youth that he could work anything—be it carpentry, milling, metallurgy, and even animal husbandry, so when he came under the magnate's employ, he sometimes passed within eyesight of the master's offspring. Melisha was sixteen, innocent, and in love with horses, so when she found Androni breaking one of her father's stallions, she engaged him in conversation. The afternoon rolled into night and the next day she sought him at the wheat fields. From there, they spoke often and each day when she completed her lessons at the house, she'd seek him wherever he had been assigned. This went on for weeks until a change came upon the family in the way of a competing farm.

The two properties abutted one another, and although each man owned thousands of hectares, each wanted to own the other's fields. Part of the subterfuge between the dynasties revealed itself in the respective foremen stealing away the best workers. The Acsad Clan, Melisha's side and the man who Androni labored for, took the Magyar Clan's head farrier. In response, the Magyar foreman came in the night to steal away Androni by force. It was at the new master's farm that Androni discovered racism.

He had been raised by people much like himself in appearance, but this family was much more Arian, light skin, light eyes, and high cheekbones. Androni's questionable parentage and obvious ethnic shortcomings brought him abuse in his new home.

Plus, he missed Melisha. More than that, she missed him, and within a month, they discovered ways to meet on the property line when no one would notice. Melisha did not see his swarthy appearance as a detraction and Androni decided he would make her his wife. He had paid very little attention to the politics of the country, and chose to ignore that the agricultural elite would determine his commingling with their daughter to be the enormous issue that it was. All Androni knew was here was a person who could complete him, *because every man is half a man until he finds a wife,* a phrase Androni learned along the way and he believed it.

When Melisha revealed that she wanted him too, he waited to collect his wages, and in the dark of night, he snuck her away from the quiet manor. By the time her parents awoke to find them gone, he was three towns away and still moving, carrying them across the border to his hometown. None of his employer's people knew of Androni's beginnings so he figured that there, they should be safe. Once they had settled in Halasto, Androni made her his wife.

Is that why I lost her? Did I cause this?

Standing in the vestibule of Corescu's old house, Androni frowned at that memory fragment. He had stolen away their princess. Was it any wonder that three weeks later, a band of marauding pillagers took her out of his bed and had him bound, gagged, and blindfolded, stuffed in a cart and driven through the night only to be dropped into a hole to die?

Androni recalled that night, too. He had hit hard ground, bruised but unbroken, and when no help came, he dozed in wait. He later awoke to a fire at his throat, a vicious attack of dual knives before the unbelievable sensation of something sucking blood directly from his neck. The suction was more frightening than the pain of the claws digging into his upper arms. In his terror, he lost consciousness.

When he came-to, he was free of the bindings, his gag no longer in place. The sunlight streamed into the hole, drawing a bright white circle on the dirt floor. He climbed carefully up and felt stronger than ever in his life, as if invigorated by a long nourishing sleep. He crawled to the lip of the hole to look about and did not recognize the landscape. The mountain range was on the wrong side and the trees were more needled than leafed. The position of the sun informed it was almost noon and Androni shimmied out of the hole to sit on the edge, his legs hanging in the darkness.

Suddenly, nausea hit his middle. Androni tolerated it, believing it would pass; after all, he had just been attacked. His hand went to his throat. No wound. Had that been a dream? Androni's mind processed these things as the nausea grew. The sun did not provide the warmth and comfort it should. Instead, each beam of light caused worse distress. Finally, he could take it no more and Androni slipped his body back into the dark cave.

He was restored! Renewed!

But why would the sunlight give me such trouble?

The ridiculousness caused Androni to again poke his head out the hole. He was consumed with sickness worse than before. The scientific deduction was complete—the sun made him ill. Androni pondered these things for so long that when he poked out his head again, the nauseating orb was hidden below the horizon. The night air caressed his skin and it felt glorious. He fairly wanted to jump for joy. Coming to his feet on the forest floor, Androni's legs yearned to run. Starting at a slow jog, he picked up the pace with the resurgence of joy and happiness growing inside. Then, he was running so fast that the landscape blurred. This frightened him into slowing down and he did, coming to a stop in a small clearing.

And I am not even winded!

What had happened to make him so alive? Androni turned a circle and palpated his chest, his torso, his arms. Something had happened to him overnight. He was different. He'd always been trim but now his muscles were hard, like those of an athlete in the Olympiad.

A deer appeared, saw Androni, and took off. Androni watched the moving branches in its wake and wondered when he'd last eaten. He had no idea how long he'd been in the cave with that monster, but his stomach roiled now. Venison might be nice. Androni followed the deer with his eyes, the landscape lit with a special light, every object illuminated with a bright aura of varying shades of blue and white. Androni squinted, seeing clearly, and followed the progress of the galloping animal.

I could catch that deer... I could fashion some sort of weapon or spear. I could make a fire an eat fresh venison tonight!

Androni's mind cheered at his thoughts and without wasting another moment, he zoomed forward with the same speed he discovered moments ago. The deer's slender neck was in his grip in an instant. With nothing but his hands to work with, Androni squeezed and its neckbones fractured.

What strength! he thought as the animal's head flopped lifeless to one side.

Then Androni experienced a duality, one that never occurred after this night. His stomach imagined the deer roasting over a spit, but his brain sought the red fluid that powered the animal's heart. A strange itching sensation tickled his gums. Still holding the deer with one arm as if it weighed nothing, Androni's finger went to his mouth. His teeth were longer. One check and they were pointed. Then, with no planning, but to satisfy an urgency he'd never experienced before, Androni bit into the animals hide with his sharp new teeth. The power and force he used brought forth the animal's blood in much more volume than he could handle. Red liquid filled his mouth, poured down his chin, down his chest, all the way to the ground. He drank until he could pull no more and then dropped to his knees, the pleasure of the meal closing his eyes. The deer dropped to the wet earth.

Something had happened in the cave. Agility, speed, bloodthirst, fangs... aversion to sunlight. Androni's people knew the legend of the vampire. His people knew to stay in the light and make the sign of the cross.

• • •

Standing in the vestibule of the borrowed property, Androni considered the dark ceiling.

Maybe Melisha had loved Androni Miklos. *Maybe.* She certainly held great affection for him. But she was

118

never seen again and Androni lived on, learning the rules on his own. Once he discovered how to swoon his victims, he did not kill them. Before he met the Ghost, he did not allow anything to cause him distress. He would always have food, shelter, and the adoration of all who knew him. He loved the audience. He loved their worship. He *did not like* discomfort or dissatisfaction.

But now he was unhappy every hour.

"But he told you I love you."

Androni's skin prickled. Even in the places a vampire doesn't have sensations, from his head to his toes, his hair stood on end.

"That is not what I want," Androni said with his mouth. But his heart peeked inside and his ears perked listening for more. They said to the voice of their own accord, *tell me more about this love.*

Androni's mouth said, "stay away from me." But even addressing the God of the universe was a bad idea. Androni covered his mouth and closed his eyes and waited for Joey to emerge.

15 | The Sneak

Arise, O God, judge the earth;
For You shall inherit all nations.
Psalm 82:8

ANDRONI'S PATIENCE RAN THIN, so after five minutes, he strode to the closed door. He focused on the voices, but they muffled through the wall, leaving him unable to distinguish the words. At first this was not alarming, maybe Corescu had used a special construction method that caused this. But when Androni sent his mind to the place he normally found the Ghost, a wall had been erected. Frowning, he focused on the room door, where on the opposite side, the preacher spoke with his only friend. He could go back in, it wasn't locked. Even if it was, he would have no trouble pushing through. Why didn't he go in and stop this, whatever was happening?

"But he told you I love you."

The voice would not give up. Was Tony's God muzzling their conversation? Preventing Androni from going in?

This is exactly what's happening. God took offense at vampires, so he took offense at Androni.

But he told you that I… love… you…

The voice slowed and spaced the last three words. This was not Androni's imagination or memory of something he heard. This was an *entity* speaking directly to Androni.

"What do you want from me?" Androni whispered,

afraid to speak telepathically with a specter he couldn't verify.

"To know how much I love you..."

It was too much. No one loved Androni but the Ghost and this voice represented a lie. No matter how much his heart scolded him for his attitude, his brain instructed him to go, get away from the preacher, and run from this God they worshiped.

Androni stepped to the main entry hall. The double front doors beckoned, but he paused to listen. Upstairs on the opposite end of the huge home, the woman was speaking to someone, probably on the phone by the cadence of the speech. Androni only cared about her as far as her blood would go and he did not want her to come out of the room and see him. He turned for the exit.

I will stretch my legs, check the perimeter, clear my head...

Androni put his hand to the knob not wanting to leave Ghost solely in the care of Agricola. He wanted to get out, to run, to get away from the preacher, and get away from that voice. But to get away from the Ghost?

No!

Androni instead pressed his back against the doors, facing the staircase and still listening to only mumbling from where the preacher spoke to Joseph. If he left, he was leaving Ghost.

Cursing with every profanity he had learned in his long life, Androni whipped around and exited the house. On the porch, he pressed both doors closed and affixed the bolt with telekinesis to protect his friend from intruders as he walked the property. He stepped to the edge of the half-circle porch supported by four chipping columns and considered the lawn. He peered across the overgrown landscape at what undoubtedly used to be meticulously manicured by the doctor's staff, but it had grown waist-high with every known species of wild grass. Blending perfectly with the forest barely twenty yards away, the woods would eventually take over the house.

Androni descended three brittle steps to the ground and turned his face to the black sky, taking in the full moon and stars in the millions. Everything glowed as beautiful as always in his vampire vision and his mind raced over his choices.

Kill the preacher; Ghost will forgive me over time…

Take Ghost away from here and leave the mortals behind. Hide and run and see if God will let us be…

And the last choice seemed the only one that was unmentionable.

Listen to the preacher and the Voice.

Interrupting his unhappy thoughts, Androni caught the sound of a human heartbeat in the trees to his right. Remembering they were on the run and in hiding, he hopped into the shadows of the house and concentrated on the source. His body went on alert, ready to kill to protect what was his.

Yes, I will end anyone who threatens my union with my Ghost…

Anyone.

The private investigator. The woman. Even the preacher if need be. Androni turned his mind wholly to the man in the trees and his nails extended. He was ready.

Tailing the preacher had been easy enough. He traveled under his own name and Andy's access to the law enforcement database, not to mention his helpful comrades back at the precinct, gave him all the details of anywhere his credit card or name were used. Because Bob Ellerslie informed him via text that the man had left to find the boy, Andy accepted the added challenge.

"Agricola's wife told JoAnn that he went to bring Joey back himself, but screw that crap! He's one of them! They spoke of a

circus. Start there and GET TO MY BOY FIRST!" the text read, and Andy did his best.

When he found the circus, the preacher was already there, arriving by cab minutes before Andy parked his rented Jeep in the Karneval public parking. He had watched Agricola wander about until nightfall when a woman he recognized as Mrs. Hope Brannen pulled her car to his position and engaged him in conversation. He watched the duo speak, maybe arguing, and then she leaned against her car and Agricola walked to a tiny caravan in the woods.

Andy watched all this from a safe distance through his binoculars and when the woman toddled the same direction and also went into the trailer, Andy jogged to her car, attached a tracking device to the underside of her bumper and jogged out of sight. By the time he reached his original hiding spot, Agricola emerged from the trailer with none other than Joseph Ellerslie and the magician who allegedly took him away in the first place.

From the four of them walking to the woman's car, Andy pondered how to separate the runaway boy from the others. His fear of monsters had all but faded; since he arrived in country, the case proceeded as normal as anything, and Agricola, Brannen, the magician, and Joseph did not present him with any measure of trepidation. They drove away as Andy snuck unseen to his own car, allowing the GPS device to give them a good head start. Waiting in his car, Andy watched vehicles arrive and exit the fairgrounds. When the GPS readout revealed Agricola had reached the city outskirts, he left the fairgrounds.

It had worked perfectly. The target traveled an hour westward and stopped at a dilapidated hidden manor. They were well settled in when Andy crept his 4-wheel-drive Jeep a hundred yards from the broken house to situate himself in the trees on the east end.

From his makeshift tree stand, which he fashioned

from a strap he'd brought in his pack for this purpose, Andy had an unobstructed view of the entire front and east end of the house. He trained his binoculars to the second-floor corner room where the woman paced around, speaking on the phone, the space illuminated by a flickering light Andy guessed to be a kerosene lantern. She preened and flipped her hair as she spoke and once, she came to the window facing Andy and looked into the night. She wouldn't see him, but she scanned the area once and turned, still speaking into her cell.

Andy sighed. He might have to move. The men were nowhere in sight and that meant they were likely on the opposite end of the house. He calculated his best method of crossing the lawn to see into the other windows when his movement caused a branch to break. Andy froze. The owls hooted, the sound of insects singing filled the air, but nothing moved. In slow motion, he worked himself down from the tree and leaned against it, his eye on the front doors.

I could go around back...

The position of the full moon caused a greater shadow in the rear of the house and he craned his head from current position.

Yeah... find an open window...

A movement at the front door grabbed his attention. The shape of a man, first not even a silhouette, just a possible head-shaped shadow. And then, he stepped to the moonlit porch. It was the magician.

Inside he scolded himself. *I must have lost my mind thinking this has something to do with vampires. Gah, Andy, geesh...*

Remaining perfectly still, Andy watched the magician look up to the sky.

He's just an eccentric European, a friend of Tony's. His wife said as much. I'm sure if I walk up there and ask to see the kid, they'll let me in...

But if that was so, why had they hidden in this invisible house? Ellerslie's cult theory returned to mind. "Don't trust Agricola!" the man had insisted. Could it be a cult? Had this man and Tony brainwashed the kid? The evidence leaned that way, mostly because of the way they *hid*. It wasn't kosher.

If an eighteen-year-old boy didn't want to go home, he doesn't have to hide.

Sure, Bob had acquired legal documentation from the German constabulary to bring Joseph by force if necessary, but surely the kid would come before it went that far.

Andy's right hand went to his gun. He'd been issued a permit, limited as it was, but he shouldn't have to use it. This wasn't a kidnapping case so much as a runaway. The more he thought about it, watching the man on the lawn looking up at the stars, he figured Bob Ellerslie had been hysterical.

But I still need to bring their son home. Let the boy duke it out with his folks there, in Montgomery.

Andy needed to get Joseph Ellerslie into his car.

Maybe I could start by subduing the magician, Andy thought. *Handcuff him, render him harmless, and then go inside, confront Agricola, and take the boy.*

Andy unlatched his holster and the man in the yard turned his head. He hadn't made a sound, the soft leather quiet as a mouse. The man turned his body and their eyes locked.

No, it's an illusion. He can't see me. I'm in complete darkness. He'd need night vision goggles to see me in here!

Andy's mind raced as he worked the problem. And then the man was gone.

Just like the doctor the night he killed the monster, Rakha Tep.

Andy's blood ran cold.

Maybe he leapt aside. Maybe I blinked. Maybe it's a trick of the light.

125

Andy hugged his back to the tree, his eyes wide. His right hand found the butt of his pistol and he thought to pull it free of the holster. Before he did, in the space of milliseconds, the weapon was yanked from his side, tossed, and cool hands encircled his throat.

"You must be the private investigator," a voice asked close to his ear from behind.

Andy leapt into action, attempting to drop low and escape, but the hands followed, and as his movements pulled his back from the tree, now the man pulled their bodies together and the hands dropped to wrap Andy up in a chest-squeezing hug. He could not breathe, the magician's arms feeling more like steel than muscle, constricting and tightening the more he worked to be free. Andy stomped at the man's feet and missed and lifting a heel to his groin did not make contact.

He was passing out.

He couldn't breathe.

He decided to ask for mercy.

"Please... don't... I can't breathe," he whispered, barely making a sound. The contact lessened and he took in a ragged lungful of air, still held firmly to the magician's chest.

"Is that better?" the smooth accented voice asked.

Andy nodded and whispered thank you.

"Are you here to take my Ghost away?" the magician asked still against his ear.

Andy wondered at the man's angle. Was he in danger? Was this man a killer? How far did this cult go when it came to protecting their interests? Andy gave a half-truth to see if it would work.

"I'm Andy Kranchez," he rasped, still recovering from the earlier compression. "I was hired to bring Joseph home."

"But the boy belongs to me," the man said and lowered his head until his lips brushed the skin beneath Andy's earlobe. "I could never let you take him away..."

Andy had no response and the man's chest fluttered with a deep inhale. Just when he thought he might be released, the mouth opened against his skin. Andy's heart exploded with fear, recalling how Tep attacked poor Bailey in the very same way.

Then came the stab—twin icepicks into his throat.

This can't be real! his mind shouted but Andy couldn't scream. The steel bands around his chest resumed their suffocating hold and Andy closed his eyes to the pain. His attacker's lips remained, impossibly suctioning the skin, pulling Andy's blood like in a Hollywood movie. Through a fog of pain and fear, Andy considered his options. He needed to live, he needed to survive. Then he thought of his son and his heart swelled with grief.

"Please don't kill me," he whispered, the thought of Billy orphaned without warning filling his mind with sorrow. Billy was high-functioning, but the Down's could prevent him from comprehending his father's disappearance. Andy added with tears in his eyes, "Please, I have a son. He needs me. I haven't made arrangements..."

Would the man even care? Was it a man?

Andy, he's biting your neck. He's drinking your blood. This is a monster, this is not a man or the leader of a cult...

Andy barely registered when the man ceased the attack, pressing a hot tongue to the wound before replacing that with two fingers, holding Andy bodily up with one strong arm. Then he heard in his ear, "Why did you risk your life, cross the globe, to bring back a boy you don't know when your death causes suffering for the one you do?"

"I-I-I didn't expect... I didn't know I would die." Andy was passing out and he fell silent.

"I cannot allow you to take the Ghost," his attacker whispered. "I cannot allow anyone to take him. Not you, not the preacher. Not even God."

God? Andy puzzled. *What? What?*

But he heard and said nothing else. The vampire released his body and on the way to the ground, Andy asked Jesus to comfort Billy; it was about to be a very lonely life for his favorite boy.

16 | The Attack

Into Your hand I commit my spirit;
You have redeemed me, O Lord God of truth.
Psalm 31:5

THE MAGICIAN EXITED THE HOUSE, stood in the yard a few minutes, looked left and right, and disappeared. Had he vanished like he did on stage? Carle wouldn't let that distract him. The man had left the house. Now only the accountant and the woman remained between him and the serious boy.

After one last check of the perimeter, Carle skirted the scrubby yard hugging the woods and sidled against the building in a matter of seconds, the moist leaves muffling his progress. Carle conformed his back to the wall and peered over his shoulder into the nearest window. If he could inch around to the back and find an entry to the house and surprise the accountant and the boy, he may be able to claim his prize without the woman even aware of what was going on.

Carle pushed through the brambles threatening the stone walls until he reached the porch, and when he pushed the back door, it opened. This was going to be easy and Carle grinned.

The men hadn't paid her any mind since they arrived. Everything with Anthony was so urgent and serious and none of them saw what was right in front of their face. Hope could help; all they had to do was ask. Why were they so selfish? Why was Anthony so concerned about what Androni and that boy did with their lives? They ignored her questions and they ignored her advice. All the way to the hiding place, nothing she said got through. Anthony talked without end about how important it was for Androni to understand God. Hope shook her head. *Why is Anthony so wrapped up in everybody else's business?*

Hope checked her watch. They had been at the house for over an hour. The room she'd chosen was the cleanest she'd seen and had shelves of curiosities she enjoyed examining. That done, she'd phoned Ana to check on her horse. Now she was bored and Tony hadn't called her to join them.

Hope touched the thick carved corner of the deeply varnished wood bed frame. The room could have been a woman's with how meticulously it was decorated, but having known Paul, Mark's long-time housemate, she could see him living here.

She turned her gaze to the door. She'd flipped the bolt in case the P.I. came and started trouble. It was a silly precaution, but Anthony's worry was sincere.

But who's to say I'm not violently assaulted while they play preacher vs. vampire on the other side of the house?

Why hadn't they checked on her? Why weren't they more concerned for the female in their midst? Weren't they on the run from a disturbed private investigator?

Am I the only one being practical?

Hope strode to her door with purpose and yanked it wide. She looked into the dark hall.

Heck, I've waited long enough, she thought and returned to grab the lantern Anthony found plus her flashlight. Once she stepped from her room, she lifted the lantern to eye level and trained her beam down the hall toward the staircase. Anthony's voice mumbled from downstairs and she stepped forward. Imaginary rats and mice, roaches and spiders, ran at her from the black corners and Hope switched to walking double-time for the stairs. Being an outdoorsy barn girl, she wasn't normally so jittery, but this house... it was so... dead... quiet.

At the top of the staircase, Hope shined her beam to the floor below. No one in sight. Cursing under her breath, she descended to the dusty floor of the grand entry hall. The sounds of conversation were more evident but she still could not pick apart individual words. Hope spun a tiny circle considering what to do next. Behind her an open door appeared to lead to a kitchen.

Maybe this is one of my houses...

Hope hadn't memorized her own list but she knew each item on Elizabeth Hawkins'. This property was not on it. Hope grinned. It could just as well be hers. She turned to the kitchen and walked inside.

Lifting her lamp up high, the flame's light reached the countertops but not the high ceilings. The appliances were grand and plentiful but obviously from the 1970s. Because there was no power, she didn't dare look inside the refrigerator or cabinets. But in an open decorative corner shelf, she spied a beautiful bone China tea set. She headed over to examine it when a movement caught her eye. Hope flicked her gaze over; had it been in there? An apparent solarium attached to the kitchen and presumably opening to the backyard.

I bet this place was amazing when Mark lived here...

Part of her wanted to daydream about the past, but the movement reoccurred, several feet away from where she thought she saw it before. And this time, it shimmered near the door.

What could be moving out there? A bird? It had been eye-level, whatever it was, but she had only seen movement, nothing discernable. Hope lifted her lantern, staring hard at the windows inserted in the door. It was black out there, and when she moved her lantern that way, the light only bounced back without penetrating the glass.

You have a flashlight, stupid, she thought and pointed the beam out the door.

A huge man!

Hope screamed and bolted in the other direction, but the sound of crashing and stomping behind her was preceded by an incredible shove to her upper back. Hope hit the floor face first, her lantern shattering and her flashlight clattering out of reach. Then an incredible weight pressed into her back and a nasty cloth was shoved into her mouth. Hope struggled, flailing her arms and legs as if swimming on the filthy floor, but nothing changed. The man was squishing her like a bug. Hope screamed into the gag and had the presence of mind to yank it out. Before she pushed anything from her lips, the man shoved it in again and pinned her arms, the knee coming off to hold her wrists in the small of her back.

She had to get free, where was Anthony?

"Be still or I will kill you!" the man hissed.

Hope stopped struggling, but she did not give up.

Blasted woman!

The American equestrienne was petite but strong; if she hadn't stopped squirming this last time, Carle would have finished her off. But she obeyed his order and stilled. This was good. He had to think. Carle had never killed a woman. In fact, besides this moment, he had only been this close to a female three times. The first time, he had received unwanted attention from an older cousin at his bar mitzvah. He had just turned thirteen when she grabbed his crotch with one hand and his neck with the other and forced her tongue into his mouth. He never told anyone and she never did it again. End of that story. But it may have affected him later because by the time he was seventeen, he still hadn't found a girlfriend. His father thought he should learn from a pro and hired a prostitute. This woman came to the house, slept in his room, and left after midnight. When Carle did not return his father a good report, he called for another. When the second woman left and his father asked how it went, Carle made up a proper story. From then on, Benedict found his son fit for duty and left him to his own love life.

Good, Carle snarled. He loved his papa and cherished his memory, but that had been tough, dealing with those *huren.*[9] He never sought female companionship of any fashion after that, and until his father died, his focus was learning the family business. Only when the laughing boys took his father away did he switch his energy to settling the score.

The American could hardly breathe and she was *so small.* He hadn't realized this until now, never having been this close to her at the riding center. He felt nothing for her; she represented an obstacle to gaining the serious boy. Carle listened to her struggling to breathe. He could kill her, he was able. She was almost gone anyway.

She went limp.

Carle released her wrists and rolled her onto her back. Her face had lost its color and her eyes were at half-mast. Was she dead? He checked her pulse at her neck. There might have been a thump, but he was no doctor.

She's out of the way. That's what I need, Carle thought and took hold of her forearms. Standing tall he dragged her to a closed door in the wall. It was a pantry, dusty spider webs on the shelves and broken boxes of long-

---

[9] Whores (German)

dissolved food on the tile. He folded the woman's tiny form inside and closed the door. The edge featured a drop-lock and he flipped it. If she came to, he'd probably hear her before she escaped.

So now... *the serious boy.*

It was only three strides to the doorway and Carle covered the distance without a sound. Peering into the darkness, he wished he had grabbed the woman's flashlight, but he needed to keep moving. Another five strides and he saw the closed door. Moonlight lay across the forgotten stone floor in a wide swath pouring through curtainless windows. There would be enough light to navigate. Carle reached for the knob.

This is where the accountant is speaking to the serious boy...

All Carle needed to do now was overcome the weakling accountant and grab his prize. Taking a deep breath, he surged forward to burst in. In the same moment, the door swung in and the stranger with the goatee walked out. The two men collided, the smaller man's face erupting into a mask of surprise.

"Oh! Sorry! Who are you?" the man exclaimed, with interest, not fear or suspicion. He attempted to help Carle find his balance with gentle hands to his either arm.

Carle reached for his bat.

Yanking it from its holster, he backed from the American and swung the club, striking the man across the temple. In an instant, the man's eyes glazed and he collapsed to the floor, twitching. Carle raised his gaze to see the pale boy heading over with eyes as round as saucers.

"Oh God!" the boy yelped and dropped to his knees at the downed man's side. "Help! Androni!" the boy yelled and put his fingers to the fallen man's throat.

Carle swiveled his gaze to the dark space behind him. Was the magician nearby? He'd seen him leave the house, but he might have returned. No time to plan,

Carle hiked back his arm and swung the bat a measured degree across the boy's downturned cranium. Without a sound, the boy's weight dropped forward. He was out. Checking behind him once more, Carle grabbed the boy, lifting him upward to wrap around his chest, and he dragged him, walking backward into the kitchen.

I will take him out the back… I'll get him in my car…

Carle was halfway across the kitchen when the boy moaned.

Good… I must not have hurt him too bad… he's coming to. This is very good!

Carle grinned, he had much more to do. He hadn't gotten his thrill and he needed that payment for it to count. The boy groaned, this time a discernible word.

"Androni…"

Ah, that pained voice! Carle's body began to hum, the same sensation he received when he ended the laughing boys. It was time to collect at least a portion of his reward.

Right here? Right now? he asked himself and knew the answer. It had to be now. He would follow his instincts, which right now demanded he begin his work on the serious boy without delay. Decided, he lowered his prize to the dusty floor in the beam of the woman's discarded flashlight.

Oh, he was beautiful. His skin so smooth—he probably didn't even yet shave. Carle placed him on his back, straightening his arms and legs. With one more quick glance around, he focused on the young man's face. He was barely conscious, a small pool of blood had seeped beneath his head, but no longer bled. He turned glazed and half-open gray eyes to Carle's direction, parting his lips, pale and barely pink.

The magician kissed him there.

Carle moistened his own lips at the memory. He hated those women who slimed his mouth all those years ago and he hadn't desired to kiss afterward. But a new sensation crawled up his spine, feathering across his jaw. If he pressed his mouth to this perfect boy's, he would get his reward. Carle needed to time it perfectly and he would use his hands. Carle positioned his palms to either side of the serious boy's throat.

Oh! I knew it!

His fingers met at the back and his thumbs stroked the boy's Adam's apple. A perfect fit. A surge of adrenaline hit him anew at this realization and Carle leaned down.

The timing.

The squeeze and the kiss.

This would be his new life.

His new mission, and it was *so* much better than the one before. Where his first calling had been to find justice for his father's murder, this mission was for Carle and Carle alone. He would cherish every kill, find them, stalk them, and earn this moment—the opportunity to squeeze until he absorbed their lives.

The mere thought of choking this gorgeous young man sent waves of pleasure throughout Carle's body. He would wait no longer. Closing the distance, he touched his fevered mouth to the boy's lax lips and squeezed his fingers.

He had chosen correctly. This was what he needed. And it was so… very… perfect.

Joey's call for help pierced Androni to the core. Sprinting across the landscape, Androni cursed himself for wandering such a distance away. When he reached the porch, he kicked in the door with power and skidded to a stop in the grand entry. His ears and heart sought his other half and he picked up the aroma of blood. Looking right, he found the preacher bleeding and unconscious on the floor outside the room they'd been speaking in. Before he could move to help, a crash from the next room called him to enter.

In the dilapidated kitchen, an enormous stranger had positioned himself over the Ghost. With a shout of rage, Androni shoved the stranger hard and surged into him, lifting him off the ground. Even as the attacker recognized what was happening, Androni threw him bodily across the kitchen. He hadn't used these skills in a decade, his life more about peace and voluntary blood. But he had not lost his power; the tall stranger slammed against the far wall and crumpled to the floor, dazed.

Androni swiveled and dropped to Joey's side, his eyes flitting between Ghost and the attacker. He checked Joey's injuries; they were healing and he was coming around. Androni lifted him to a sitting position, but in his peripheral vision, the attacker rolled to his knee and then his feet across the room. Androni would need to end him. Positioning Joey against the wall, Androni faced the maniac. The stranger felt along the dark counter, his fingers skirting the surface as Androni assumed a crouch, ready to strike. Then the man swung his right hand into view brandishing a rusty carving knife. He surged toward Androni, lumbering close enough for an evil swipe. Androni deflected the blow, but it came again and again. Androni parried unhurt, seeking an opening to attack. He needed to get close enough to grab the man's neck.

I can twist off his head, but I must… get… closer…

Androni could take a stab wound. It had been years, but he knew how quickly such an injury would heal. If he allowed the man to stab him, he'd be close enough to grab his neck. Decided, Androni checked Joey with a quick peek—he was growing stronger but still could not stand—and he leapt into the maniac's space.

When Andy returned to consciousness, the first thing he did was check his throat. Careful palpation with two fingers found it had scabbed with minimal trauma. He then concentrated on his overall body—his breathing was fine, he had no pain, he was okay. Had the magician purposefully left him alive? Amazed, Andy got to his feet, grabbed his bag, picked up his discarded weapon, and stumbled toward the car. The shortest distance would be across the front lawn. He would have to pass near the front doors. The front windows. With a new brave face, he scooted across the weedy yard, wire-like reeds whipping his slacks.

Halfway there, a commotion from inside the house reached his ears and then a call for help. It had been faint, but had it been the boy? Andy froze in place, crouching and thinking fast. The image of the youngster in danger tugged his conscience. He was well. God had saved him from whatever happened in the trees. Was it because he still had a role to play in the drama God created this night?

"I'm here. I'm fine. I think You're telling me to help…"

With that small prayer in his heart, Andy headed for the doors. They sat on broken hinges and his hand went to his gun. He balanced it in his shooting hand, his finger to the side of the trigger, and crossed the threshold. Going into police mode, he took cover against the wall. Training his beam left and then right, he discovered the inert form of Agricola on the filthy floor. Andy saw no one else around and he jogged close, eyes jumping for any surprises.

"Tony! Are you okay! Hey," he whisper-shouted, nudging the man's shoulder hard. Agricola gurgled but did not awaken. Andy checked his pulse. It was strong. In a nearby room to his left, a new sound rumbled. The woman? The boy?

Agricola was in dire straits.

Decision made, he holstered his gun and grabbed

the man under the armpits. As he'd been trained in the Army, medic-style, he dragged Tony across the floor to the grand hall. When he reached the destroyed double exit doors, a shadow swished passed, bumping into him before continuing into the house. Tucked under his arm, Andy's flashlight shone to the floor, so he did not see who or what slipped by. Andy had to keep moving. Trusting God saw everything he could not, Andy focused on getting Tony to the car.

At the Jeep hidden in the overgrown vegetation, he carefully lay Tony across the backseat.

"Joseph," the man mumbled, his eyes still closed. "Is he okay?"

"Hush," Andy said in an urgent hiss. "Stay here. I'll get him. Stay down." The Jeep's First Aid kit sat attached to the back of the front seat and Andy slapped it open. Among the items that tumbled out was a roll of gauze. As tidy as a wartime doctor, he wrapped Tony's head and checked his pulse. The guy would live. Now he needed to find the Ellerslie boy.

Asking God for strength, Andy closed the car door with Tony inside and faced the house. His hand went to his holster. His gun was gone.

It had been a good idea in theory. Androni grabbed the stranger's throat, making it possible for the man to embed his knife in Androni's middle. The plan to twist off the guy's head as soon as this happened went askew when the stranger withdrew his knife and inserted it again.

Umph umph umph in rapid succession, the killer thrust his knife into Androni's middle. The strength Androni required to resist melted away with every new jab. Androni's hands came up in defense and his palms met the cruel blade as well. Androni tumbled to the floor under the man's weight, wondering at his egregious error. He had very little experience with aggressive interactors and his paucity was about to kill him.

Then, as he had often heard might happen, Androni's life flashed before his eyes. He stopped the review at Joseph Ellerslie, the boy he loved with his entire heart. Androni's face fell to the side and he sought Ghost's eye. His attacker had finally ceased repetitive action and leaned on the knife, embedded between two ribs, although Androni felt only the pressure of the weight.

"I love you, please don't die" the boy sent to his mind, red-tinged tears streaming down his face. The boy wanted to move, to help, to come, but he hadn't recovered enough to react.

Androni gave him a tiny grin, ignoring the maniac over him, still pushing into his knife. *"You are wonderful to me,"* he sent to the boy's mind, recalling in an amazing rush their every moment together. The night they met— the boy coming down the stairs at Mark's request, meeting Androni's eye the first time. *I loved him then...* Later that same night, they talked of plans, of the future, of how to truly live. *"I never wanted to live so much until I met you, beautiful boy... You gave me life..."*

"Androni, please, fight, please..."

Even Joey's telepathic voice was weak and Androni attempted to soothe him with his gaze. He couldn't stop it now, he would die. What would that be like?

"Jesus loves you, Androni, don't forget..." his beloved sent, holding his gaze in the special light of their vampire vision. *"As Him to help you. He doesn't want you to die like this... I promise. Ask..."*

Androni did not understand what his Ghost meant—die like how?

"Unbelieving," Joey sent, new tears trickling from both eyes.

"Don't cry, beloved, I will ask. I will ask now." Androni

closed his eyes, the sad smile he held for Joey fading from his mouth. A small check found the killer still hovering, immobilizing Androni with his weight. Androni recalled that insistent voice and focused down.

"You said you love me, but do You love the Ghost? Please save him, for me, for Your Androni. Thank You for putting us together. I know it was You. I love him. Thank you." Androni felt a sense of peace wash over him, much like he felt when looking into his Ghost's eyes. *"Your son Joseph doesn't want me to die. I don't know what to do or say. Just do whatever You will... I accept Your judgment."*

The cavernous old kitchen filled with the sound of cannon fire and Androni's eyes flew open. At the same time, the man pressing the knife into his left lung fell to the side. Lying flat on his back, Androni turned his face to Joey. Then, thick, strong arms lifted Androni's upper body across a masculine lap. He kept his eyes trained to Joey who also did not look away.

"I asked. I asked," Androni sent over and whomever held him pushed a bleeding wound to his mouth. Without breaking eye contact with the Ghost, Androni accepted, wrapping his mouth around a thick wrist.

"He sent help," Ghost sent over. *"Just like when I was lost. I prayed He would help you. See? He won't let you die this way..."*

Androni couldn't deny Joey was correct. The blood that filled his mouth and then stomach did its work, repairing his wounds and reinvigorating his entire system.

When his rescuer toppled over, Androni dropped the wrist, never having removed his eyes from the Ghost. Oh, he was restored. After rolling to his knees to check his condition, Androni crossed to Joey, his multiple stab wounds already closed because of the considerable donation of his rescuer. He reached his Ghost and pulled him close.

"Eli," Joey said against his cheek. "Eli. Help him."

Androni swiveled his gaze to his rescuer. His long-time roustabout lay on his side, unconscious and his large heart was losing rhythm. He had lost too much blood and his labored breathing alerted Androni that his time was nearly up. He looked at the Ghost.

"Save him," Joey whispered, his eyes filled with pain at the thought of the great man perishing after saving Androni's life.

"I will," Androni replied and grabbed his attacker's discarded kitchen knife. When he had plunged it into his arm, he did the same to Eli's inert wrist and pressed them together. Would that do it? He had never transformed a human into a vampire, but this is the way Joey said it was done to him.

Androni watched his roustabout's face and then settled onto his rump to pull Eli's head into his lap. "Eli? *A barátom…*"[10] he whispered and wiped the sweaty brow with his fingers.

Motion at the kitchen entrance caused him he and Joey both to look up.

It was the investigator and he did not look happy.

---

[10] My friend. (Hungarian)

17 | The Compromise

WHAT AM I LOOKING AT?

Andy shone his beam to the faces in the room. Farthest from his position, a dead man on his side facing away, a sizable exit wound in the back of his skull. Joseph Ellerslie, wounded, sitting against the righthand wall, looking at him with sad eyes. The magician sitting cross-legged holding in his lap one of the circus workers Andy recognized from his earlier reconnaissance.

So… he thought. *What am I looking at?*

"Did you see Pastor Tony?" the boy asked then, his voice weak. "He's hurt, please, help him."

Andy nodded, breaking himself out of his frozen state. He made a wide berth around the magician and the sleeping man in his lap and gained on the boy. Coming close, he hunkered sideways to keep the magician *(vampire? Had that happened?)* in view.

"He's good. He's in my car. He's okay. How about you? What hurts?" Andy asked, assessing and touching various points for injury.

"You're the guy my dad hired?" the boy asked and Andy nodded.

"Come on, let's get you on your feet. I think you're okay," he said and tenderly positioned his arm to help the kid stand. Joseph allowed it and once on his feet he stood on his own. Before Andy could make other suggestions, he stepped across the space to drop to the floor beside the magician *(again… didn't he attack me like a vampire?).* Andy searched the floor and his beam landed across his gun, dropped by whomever jacked it at the front door.

"Andy."

It was the magician. Andy met his eye, his mind calculating the effort required to leap for his pistol.

"Andy, don't."

The man's smooth voice matched his tone from the trees, but this time, Andy faced him. He sat in the beam of a flashlight slung to the floor, but Andy could see the man's eyes. Clear, friendly, in an amazing face—he hadn't noticed from his earlier distance, but he looked like a nice guy, a good guy, a man who this boy obviously cared about…

Joseph maneuvered his shape to eclipse the magician's form, as if protecting him from Andy.

Was I being hypnotized? he wondered and tried to clear his head.

"Take Pastor Tony to the hospital, Mr. Kranchez," the boy said, his back turned. "Hurry. We're okay here."

Andy's eyes returned to the gun. He really should bring Joseph, too. The boy swiveled his face to Andy's, reddish tears in his bright gray eyes.

"Andy," he said in a different voice from before, smooth, flat and emotionless, "take Tony to the hospital. Now."

Andy nodded and stepped backward to the kitchen door. "I'll take Tony to the hospital," he said and flit the beam to the dead man and back to the cluster of magician, circus worker, and Joseph Ellerslie. "You guys are okay?"

"We are fine. Tony's in danger, though," the boy said in the same voice.

Andy offered a nod and backed another step.

"You're not in a cult? You're just... you have a new family?" Andy asked, working up a story that might still get him paid and allow the Ellerslies to drop their drastic measures. *If Joseph simply picked a new family, a new partner, hell... the Ellerslies can work that out...*

Andy tipped to the right and his eye landed in Androni's on Joseph's other side.

But regular magicians don't have fangs and drink blood.

"I'm not in a cult. I'm with Androni. Tell them. I'm going to be a magician. Tell them I'll start writing, I promise."

Andy backed again, and now stood in the hallway. "You're not in danger..."

Joseph sighed, shook his head and turned to face his friend.

Andy had seen enough. Feeling a nudge from his God, he shuffled out the front door and jogged to the Jeep. Running over everything he'd seen and experienced *(I have holes in my neck...)*, he checked Agricola and found him stable. He'd leave Joseph here, trust the boy's words. Hell, he was eighteen, an adult. Bob Ellerslie might have a harder time hiring someone to return him by force now that Andy had testimony of the boy's safety and his explanation for leaving.

And what's that, Andy? he asked himself with snark as he navigated the broken road. *That Joseph Ellerslie meets this European magician, falls in love, and runs away with him. His parents think he's in a cult and order him to come home.*

Or...

This European vampire turned the boy into one, too, and there's no way he's coming back to plain, old, Alabama.

Andy rolled in his lips and checked on Tony with a quick peek. He was awake and trying to sit up.

"How's Joey?" he asked in a choke and situated himself against the door. He was pale but looked good considering his wound.

"He's staying with that Androni guy," Andy said,

marveling at his own words. He didn't know what to believe, but he and Agricola were safe—they were where they wanted to be. The Ellerslie boy and his …friend… were where they wanted to be.

"Okay, good," Tony answered with a slow nod. "And you'll let that be?"

"That magician did this," Andy said without planning to, tipping his chin to the right in case Tony would view his scabbed-over punctures. "Guess you know all about that, huh?"

The man rolled his eyes with a weary movement. "Let's leave them to God, eh, Andy?" Agricola took a careful breath. "I spent our last hour together talking to them about how God loves them. I think they survived so God can continue working that out."

Andy made no answer. He looked at the dark road ahead and tried not to think about that moment in the trees.

"Jonah said you have a son. How about I go back to my sweet wife and you return to Billy, and we let God do whatever He's doing here?"

"Do you think you did what He wanted? Did you accomplish your task?" Andy asked again, off the top of his head.

Agricola thought a long moment looking out to the night and then with a definitive nod, said, "Yes, yes I did. Let's leave them to it."

Andy sucked his teeth. By the time they reached the city and Tony was wheeled into the building on a gurney, Andy decided he was right. He had only one question and didn't know if asking it would pull him back in. Who was the dead guy? He wouldn't ask. Billy needed his dad and he couldn't wait to get home.

18 | The Letter

When I cry to You,
When I lift up my hands toward Your holy sanctuary.
Do not take me away with the wicked
And with the workers of iniquity,
Psalm 28:2-3

"WE HAVE TO LEAVE. They know where we are."
Joey watched for Androni's reaction. His friend still sat
on the floor with Eli's head in his lap. The man hadn't
moved, offering no sign that the vampire transfer had
taken place. Joey's misery at watching the heroic man
die stung deep.

Would God allow Eli to die in order for Androni to
live? None of this was the way Joey thought it would go,
and he turned his heart to God and asked why. Even
though he did not receive answer, he did have a reply, a
soft whisper of the Holy Spirit revealing His presence.
As if assuring Joey that his work with Pastor Tony had
not been in vain. He could speak to God and it felt
wonderful.

Androni still hadn't moved and Joey touched his
shoulder. "He's gone," Joey said, his voice soft, his eyes
begging for Androni to look his way. "I don't know why
it didn't work. I'm just… so sorry."

Androni checked the man's pulse at his throat for
the fourth time, but nothing. No heartbeat, no
respirations. Androni's lips tightened and he sighed,
looking at the man's sleeping face. "I do not understand
any of this," he said finally with a new headshake.

"We'll give him a proper burial," Joey said feeling deep inside that is was a sign of respect to put him gently in the earth. Leaving the killer to dissolve over time on the dirty floor seemed fitting, but their rescuer? His sacrifice would be honored by their gesture.

After another thoughtful moment Androni moved out from under Eli's weight with tremendous care and set him on his back, the big man's arm falling to the side as his weight settled. A folded slip of paper tumbled from a pocket on that side and Joey lifted it from the floor before it touched any spilled blood. He and Androni got to their feet as he unfolded what appeared to be stationery paper, a white sheet with a gray scrolled border. It was handwritten in an unfamiliar language and Joey handed it to his friend.

"It's in Hungarian," Androni whispered and he read it aloud.

Androni,

I was 35 and desolate, I had lost everybody. My lovely Katerine, my babies, Lyla and Oliver, taken by the plague that swept through our village. I crawled to my ancestral home in Halastro where my mama and her mama worked the fields for the landowners.

I was a Pole, the townspeople would not accept my papers, they did not believe my claim to Mama's land. I hid in her home, afraid of being seen, I slunk in the shadows, worked the land in secret, I made my way.

Mama's treasures had been stored in a box and I found her beloved mementos. Among them, rendered in oils by a master, I found Androni.

An amazing likeness, the name on the portrait read Androni Miklos, and I remembered how Mama spoke that name to me in my youth before she died. Our relative who fell in love with my far removed relative, Melisha Acsad. She conceived a child with her husband Androni before he was killed in a horrible fire. Her family helped her with the baby, and she married again.

Subsequent generations crossed the border to Poland. Here is where Eli Rota was born. When I met you that wintry night, no one could tell me you weren't Androni from my mother's treasure box. I see you are good, you picked me up in my misery and gave me a job. You were kind, you gave me respect and treated me as if we were brothers.

Androni, in a sense, we are.

I am writing this letter in case something happens to me. I have wanted to tell you for some time, but why? If you have found a way to outlive mortal man? If you siphon life off others you have never hurt anyone. I see you are good.

If you see this letter, I thank God in heaven because it means I was able to help. When you left the circus tonight, you were followed. Eli does not have a car, but by the grace of God, I was able to find you anyway.

Tell the Ghost that I honor him and everything he stands for. Tell him I agree with what he said to the ringmaster. Tell him that if I am dead, I went to that place we both know.

If I am dead, precious brother, nay, grand-father, listen to our friend the Ghost. He is wise beyond his years.

Honor and glory to you, Androni.

You made my life a better one.

~ Eli

When he lowered the letter, Androni's eyes were wet with bloody tears and Joey leaned in to grab him in a hug.

"What did you say to the ringmaster?" his friend asked in a whisper.

Joey thought back and took a guess, saying soft in Androni's ear, "The ringmaster was thanking us for bringing in so much money. He said that because of our show, he was able to get a better doctor for his son. I didn't mean to, but when he told me about it, I said, *praise the Lord*. He was surprised because of our show, I guess. He didn't think the Ghost could believe in Jesus. I think that's what Eli overheard…"

Androni gave a thoughtful nod. "Everything comes back to Jesus, doesn't it?"

"It always has," Joey offered. "From the beginning, even before Jesus came into the world, God arranged all sorts of events to be a precursor to His arrival. He wants us to believe in Him. To save us…"

"I don't understand all of that," Androni said still wrapped in Joey's arms. "But I understand what I see with my eyes. God preserved our lives tonight."

"He sure did," Joey said. "Let's give Eli his burial and get out of here."

Androni agreed with a sad nod and lifted Eli over his shoulder. Together they walked out of the kitchen, into the dark solarium and then the overgrown yard. As predicted, a garden shed retained a collection of rusted implements and both Joey and Androni selected shovels to dig a proper grave. Then with prayers of thanksgiving and worship, they released Eli to his God.

Joey and Androni faced the forest. "What now?" Joey asked. "Do we go back to the circus?"

Androni shook his head. "No, we will forge a new path. Let's begin by walking this trail."

The faded path looked to be an animal trail, possibly deer, and Joey sighed. He would write his parents like he said and they would just need to accept their son was grown. *Let them believe whatever they want, but God left us alive…*

"Yes," Androni said answering his inner thoughts. "God left us alive, so let us walk and see what He will do next." He took a step and Joey joined him, the moon mostly done with the night and the sun daring the eastern horizon. "We will figure it out together."

Despite everything, Joey smiled. Yes, and God made sure they were alive to do so. He didn't want Androni to die outside of his Father's house. Joey nodded to himself. He would do as Pastor Tony suggested. He would keep his ears open for God and when the time was right, they would move Androni inside where it was safe. For now, they walked under a blanket of stars and trusted God to lead them down His paths.

19 | The Decision

Because they do not regard the works of the Lord,
Nor the operation of His hands,
He shall destroy them
And not build them up.
Psalm 28:5

HOPE AWOKE TO THE SENSATION of tiny feet scurrying across the skin of her upper chest. In a spasm of disgust, she kicked her legs out and the doors of the pantry in which she'd been tossed burst open wide. Sunlight streamed into the small space and she looked out, squinting at the bright light reflecting off the grimy kitchen floor...

... and a man's dead body.

Hope gasped and scrambled free of the filthy cabinet. With care she tiptoed around the corpse, recognizing him as Carle from the riding center. He'd tried to kill her. Why? Hope moved toward the kitchen exit into the house, making a wide berth around pools of blood coagulated in the center of the floor.

Once in the main hall, similarly awash with sunlight, Hope called the names of her friends throughout the house. No reply. Had they really left her there? Before she grew angry, her eye fell on a significant blood pool in the doorway of the room Tony and Joey had talked in. Alarmed for her friend, Hope jogged into the yard and slid into her rental car. The keys were not in the ignition, so she locked the doors and hugged herself to think.

My phone!

She felt her back jeans pocket and thanked her lucky stars she still had it. *And it's still charged!* Hope first called Anthony and screamed with joy when he picked up the line.

"Are you okay! Oh, my God! What's going on?" she yelped.

On his end, her old friend said he was in the hospital but okay and began to give her an overview of what happened. The dead man was wanted for several murders and had been dubbed The Reaper for the papers. Anthony said when he was able, he had given the address to the police and they would arrive in minutes. This gave Hope a sigh of relief and she asked about Androni and Joey.

"They are alive, and we decided to leave them alone, me and Andy. If you can, leave them alone, too. God is doing something there. Just… see if you can let it be."

Hope wanted to be offended at his tone, but she was too weary. She promised to report back when she was home safe and made a polite goodbye.

Should I go look for them? Are they still vampires?

Hope assumed they were based upon Anthony's silly insistence she leave them be.

Maybe I should. How much energy will I waste searching for two vampires who don't want to be found? I have horses to train and competitions to win. Hope narrowed her eyes. *I should call Ana, check on Rusty…*

Hope dialed her friend. Yeah, vampires could fall in her past. After all, she had two show horses long-listed for the Olympics, and as an American training in Germany, she was a shoe-in for a medal.

Ana started a new topic and Hope let the vampires go. For now.

20 | The Lovers

You are all fair, my love,
And there is no spot in you.
Song of Solomon 4:7

Two Weeks Later

SARAH HUGGED TONY FOR A VERY LONG TIME, thanking God in her heart for sending her beloved home safe. Everything that happened to him overseas had been recounted and could now be stored away. They would move on, both feeling in their spirits that the Lord had done what he needed to do, and that the responsibility for the boys' safety and Androni's salvation had been moved into capable hands.

That was the way the Lord worked, and Sarah was happy with that. Either he was God or he wasn't, and there was nothing in between.

"You should have seen Androni's face when he looked at Joey. It was child-like, it's as if he's amazed." Her husband's gaze grew soft with the memory. "He's seeing Jesus inside that kid. He'll be okay. This is going to work. I know it."

"In God's timing, right?" she said with a new kiss to his cheek.

"But I don't want to go along with Andy's story," Tony added when she leaned out of the hug. "They're not gay, even if they were mortal, it's not like that."

Sarah nodded and their contact slid down to holding hands. "You can stand on the truth if anyone asks. But Andy needs that story to handle what he saw. We should pray for him to forget those images, forget

154

being attacked. He might be able to do like Jonah did, convince himself over time that a madman attacked him, not a vampire."

"I hope he can." Tony nodded. "Let's pray that Androni doesn't take forever. The longer he resists, the harder the circumstances become. God will not let that man go."

Sarah offered a kind smile. "We gave it over to God. We can trust Him." She waited for her husband to agree and then kissed his nose tip. "Joey will keep in touch. He sent us update number one already."

Tony reached for his phone and re-read the message. Joey informed the couple that they were safe and traveling Europe, ears open to God. Joey still hadn't taken blood from a person directly and his coded message revealed he wouldn't; he'd made a bargain with the Lord that he wouldn't drink from people and God would give him more time with Androni. Tony sighed. Joey expected Androni to die when he accepted Jesus. Would he?

God can do whatever He wants…

If Androni died, Joey would be devastated. It was sad, but as Tony did when he let Mark go… he reminded himself that he had to trust God.

He knows the end from the beginning, Tony said inside.

Sarah hugged his neck, and all was right in the world.

END, The Corescu Chronicles

Unless…

What if the author of *The Corescu Chronicles* was chased by real-life vampires because of the spiritual messages in her books?

This is the basis of Ellen's award-winning international bestselling series, *The Rabbit Saga*, beginning with "Rabbit: Chasing Beth Rider." We have inserted an except for your enjoyment.

God bless you,

Little Roni Publishers

Sign up for email alerts on Ellen's books at

https://dl.bookfunnel.com/z0c7dpe1am

Author's note: When I finished this book, Androni urged me to write what happens next. The spin-off series will be entitled, THE CORESCU LEGACY and will involve all surviving characters as the plot requires. I hope you will sign up for my newsletter so I can alert you as they are born! Book One is underway and it is currently entitled, ANDRONI. Fitting, eh? Thank you for reading!

~ Ellen

A bestselling novelist writes of vampires, unknowingly infuriating an ancient real-life race of blood-drinkers who vow to destroy her because her books endanger their way of life. One among them doubts his leaders and thinks she's innocent.
Will he help, or join the chase?

"Epic!" 5-stars Readers' Favorite Review
NINE-TIMES Winner of the 5-star Seal

"MAZE'S STORYTELLING IS FAST AND FUN, overflowing with ideas and spiritual insight." ~ Eric Wilson, author of **Fireproof,** and *Valley of Bones (The Jerusalem Undead Trilogy)*

"With all the strange powers at work in this world, THIS BOOK REVEALS THE GREATEST POWER OF ALL." Rabbi John Giddens, *ChavurahShalom.org*

#1 Top-Rated Bestseller *Rabbit: Chasing Beth Rider*

Excerpt: Biblical worldview vampire adventure, Books 1-3 appropriate for readers 12+ with PG-13 language and violence. Installments 4 & 5 for mature teen and adult for language and adult themes, still chasing the same Truth.

1 *Watch Your Back*

Beth Rider's instincts screamed foul *milliseconds* before the largest man she had ever seen leaned his incredible bulk upon her flimsy card table. The corners of the man's mouth turned down as his fierce gaze sought hers. He was a giant; even hunched above the author's table, he would be nearly seven feet standing. His skin was as black as ebony and a long, deep scar furrowed his hairline, down his temple, past his cheekbone and faded beneath his chin. Dark blue lenses shielded his eyes and he wore a scuffed black leather jacket with no insignia. A myriad of tattoos covered what she could see of his neck, the ink three shades darker than his impossibly dark flesh. Beth reminded herself to breathe as her keen observation skills took in every disturbing detail.

"Well, if it ain't Beth Rider," he rumbled in a deep voice and Beth raised her eyes.

"That's me! How are you?" she asked disguising her startle response. She had been signing books for two hours but this person did not look like a fan.

"I got a message for you," the man said looking hard at her through his Ray-Bans.

Beth straightened her back and cleared her throat, an unnamed fear welling deep down. "A message from whom?"

"From me." The huge man swished off his sunglasses and fixed his gaze on hers. His eyes were dark and hidden behind an immense brow. The sclera surrounding his black irises was yellowed and streaked with blood vessels. His giant hand snaked forward and covered her left on the tabletop.

"Watch your back!"

Words she heard even though the man's lips did not move. Beth squealed and jumped up, sending her folding chair crashing behind her. Wrapping her arms around her chest, she backed again, stumbling over her fallen chair and cursing her chosen footwear. The bookstore worked her signing into a previously established princess-themed event; the sparkling bodice of her party dress perfectly complemented a pair of low-rise heels from a long-ago wedding party. For the moment, the same shoes were the reason she continued to tip rearward, windmilling her arms twice before a Good Samaritan hopped close to stabilize her by one arm. She couldn't thank whomever it was, or even look over—the hateful gaze of the Goliath had her mesmerized.

"Miserable witch," the voice growled again, only in her mind because the man's lips did not move.

Beth put her hands to her ears. The stranger held her gaze and waited for her to react. Two store employees approached on either side, fanning her face with their hands, the helpful rescuer still grasping her upper arm.

"Are you okay? Miss Rider, what's wrong?"

Beth stared at the monster. How could they not see? Why were they not afraid of the enormous man menacing her mere feet away?

"We're sorry, sir, just a moment," one of the uniformed workers told the giant. Beth paled—they were not afraid. Had she overreacted?

"God, help me!" she whispered, looking into the face of the giant.

At that moment, the man stood off the table, tossed Beth a malicious grin, turned, and disappeared into the throng of customers.

"God!" Beth exhaled and broke free of those who held her. "I'm sorry. I'm okay. I'm fine," she began and made a polite excuse to the circle of worried faces.

Smiling, she scooted past the crowd and entered the ladies' room at a trot. Inside a private stall, she leaned against the door and collected her thoughts. Her novels attracted a plethora of diverse characters, but the dark maniac truly frightened her. Why had he focused his hate on her? Where had his vehemence originated? There had been no doubt—he had targeted her, he knew her, he had come with purpose.

How in the world did I make an enemy of that horrifying man? And why did he call me a witch? Wait... had he even said that? It was in my head, for God's sake!

Beth could not make sense of it. With a tremendous exhale, she closed her eyes clutching herself in her own arms. Part of her wanted to call her parents in Tennessee, but she resisted. Not only was she an adult now and on her own— twenty-five only a week ago—her parents were old. She had been a surprise baby, considered a miracle since both parents were fifty-five when she was born. Now in their seventies, she feared startling either without true cause. The huge bully was gone, she was safe.

I just need to calm down. Beth... Calm. Yourself. Down.

With a few additional internal pep-talks, Beth took a deep breath, and headed back to the signing table. Writing novels was fun, meeting her readers even more enjoyable; run-ins with maniacal lunatics stunk. Big time. By the time she found her seat, swished her ridiculous but beautiful crinoline-supported fairy skirt in place, her bright smile had returned. And she put the monster out of her mind. At least for now.

2 *Silly Wabbit*

The monster had him boxed in, and it wasn't even close to sunup. "GIVE IT UP, RABBIT! You don't have a chance!" he barked, his growling tenor reverberating in Schaffer's head.

"OhmyGod-OhmyGod-OhmyGod!" he whimpered in response and tiptoed faster along the corrugated tin wall. Up ahead and much too far away, the exit emptied into the dark night. The warehouse sat on the river's edge—how far from the pier was it? Maybe fifty feet once he cleared the threshold. There was a good chance he could jump into the water and swim away. Hadn't he overheard one of them say their kind abhorred open water? Schaffer didn't have time to ponder. Taking a deep breath to gather his nerve, he burst forward only to slam into the outstretched arm of his enemy after four strides.

"Oops," the monster giggled. "Down you go."

Schaffer struggled to find his feet, but the creature grabbed him by the collar and dragged him back the way they had come, his boot heels plowing the red clay.

"Silly wabbit," the monster snickered, "Come on, we have a *big night* ahead of us."

Schaffer wrestled against his attacker's grip. The thing that held him was not his master, but he was still one of *them*. A *Rakum*. A devilish miscreant with ancient roots whose strength was outdone only by his cruelty. They would be sure to punish Schaffer for the stunt he pulled against Elder Rufus.

Schaffer's futile resistance continued as they reached the monster's Dodge pickup parked in the abandoned lot. He got a glimpse of the Rakum's face—dark-skinned with an evil glint in his black eyes; Schaffer knew this one—he went by Boris.

Master Rufus's assassin!

Schaffer yelped with new fear. The Rakum were a

hundred-thousand strong; how did he end up receiving his punishment from one of the worst?

"In ya go!" The Rakum tossed him into the passenger seat, and in a matter of seconds, zip-tied his hands together. With a smirking peek into Schaffer's horrified face, he yanked the bound wrists over his head to tie to the headrest. Schaffer cried out, but only a few syllables escaped his lips before the monster shoved a greasy rag deep into his mouth.

"Where're your matches now, Rabbit? Hmm?"

Schaffer paled in terror. He had set Rufus on fire and it had been a glorious sight—but he had intended to get away... Schaffer watched with round eyes as his attacker settled into the driver's seat and turned the ignition.

"Might be fun to burn you up. See what that smells like."

Schaffer moaned with terror—this monster would do it, he had no doubt. An hour after he set Rufus aflame, he'd been captured by one of the other Elders who forced him to drink his blood, following that with, *"start running."* Schaffer had no time to wonder why he'd been released. He had made it to the edge of town before being captured by the brute in the driver's seat. As his mind raced seeking escape, an Airstream trailer emerged nestled deep in the thick forest ahead.

The Rakum hit the brakes hard and didn't bother to come around to extricate his catch. Instead, he reached in to yank Schaffer out the driver's side. The stiff plastic ties raked across his flesh and he yelped through the filthy towel as his skin gave way. His wrist bones fractured as his hands popped free of the bonds. Bleeding and crying, Schaffer was tossed over the Rakum's shoulder. He watched the weeds go by in the moonlight, his bloodied fingers dangling in his line of vision. They no longer stung, but he was too terrified to be thankful. They entered the trailer, the door closed, and he was dropped onto a tattered yellow couch. Schaffer grunted as he landed, but one glance at his wrists revealed the skin was not ripped as he had thought.

"Let the party begin," the Rakum said, rubbing his palms together and standing over Schaffer's position. "Do you know what happens to Rakum Rabbits?"

His heart pounding, Schaffer shook his head.

"We *eat* Rabbits around here. Yep. But we take our time."

His tongue pushed at the rag in his mouth and he pleaded with his eyes.

The monster drew close, stopping inches from his sweating face. "And Rufus wants to be sure you suffer."

Rufus? Present tense? Are they fireproof? Schaffer choked back a scream as the monster withdrew a knife and brought it to his chin.

"We ain't in no hurry, Rabbit. We can go all night…"

The sharp blade pressed into Schaffer's throat until it pierced the skin with stinging pain. Blood coursed from the wound and spilled out before him onto the monster's chest. But as his assailant hovered over him, an evil grin on his dark face, Schaffer felt something else entirely. The fiery pain in his neck subsided and was replaced with a peculiar tightness. The blood that spurted forcefully from his body ebbed and then ceased.

His knife wound had healed—as if he was one of them.

The marking procedure did this!

Horrified as the gravity of his situation sunk in, Schaffer violently leapt aside. The Rakum backhanded him into place and straddled him on the couch, holding him down with his body weight.

"See, Rabbit? Now you get it."

Schaffer straightened in his bonds as the monster raised the knife and slashed again, this time across the chest. Dark oxygenated blood oozed down his shirtfront and again, the pain subsided and the flow eased. Schaffer's face twisted into a mask of horror.

"Yep. That's right. We'll go on all night. And tomorrow

night. And the night after that..."

Schaffer watched as his attacker brought the bloody knife tip to his mouth and cleaned it with his red tongue.

"Oh, shit, that... is... so..." he whispered, closed his eyes and smiled. After a moment, he sought Schaffer's terrified gaze. "And Rabbit," he said with a drunken pause, "when I get tired of you, we'll have my brothers over and let them see what fun you are."

The knife rose again and plunged into Schaffer's middle. He grunted, his gag preventing him from screaming no matter how his lungs fought to expel the terror.

"We'll never get tired of you," he whispered as his gory tongue circled his lips, seemingly intoxicated by the ingestion of Schaffer's blood. The knife was thrust in again, this time into his ribs. "And you'll never die. *Never.*"

As Schaffer felt the skin tighten and knit itself together in his middle, he had no doubt that the monster was right. His punishment would go on. Schaffer was in hell and his hell would last forever.

3 *The Book*

"It's only three. You're not leaving, are you?" the handsome blond youth across from Javier asked, his eyes wide. "You haven't heard the best part."

Javier hadn't yet taken Simon's blood and the boy probably feared he might skip it. Would he? Javier licked his lips before replying. When he arrived tonight, the youth had launched into reading part of a novel and before long, they were fifteen chapters in. A grumble from Javier's middle sounded and Simon sat upright from his position on the bed.

Javier corrected him with his hand upraised, palm out. "No, read on. What happened next?"

Simon's expression relaxed. He loved giving blood but would settle for sitting under Javier's gaze a bit longer. His young friend was sharing the strangest tale Javier had ever heard and they'd only covered two-thirds of the story. He put both hands into his wavy black hair and massaged his scalp as Simon picked up where he'd left off.

With no human experience, the religious-themed plot made little sense, but Javier enjoyed the bloodthirsty nature of the main character. The storyline featured a priest who had been transformed into a vampire by the devil. The priest murdered a hapless mortal every night until the novel's protagonist, an aspiring preacher, convinces him to stop. The spiritual struggle of the protagonist intrigued Javier more than it should. Did such faith exist in the real world? Most bewildering of all, did their God *pop in* to save them as He did in this novel? Javier didn't know. In fact, he didn't know any gods. He'd never been to a church, synagogue, or temple, nor had he ever uttered a prayer in a time of need. Yet, as his favorite donor sat on his lumpy bachelor's bed, reading to him from this mortal woman's novel, something deep inside fluttered. For the first time in his long life, Javier experienced a desire to know this God. The sensation was peculiar, and he didn't resist. Instead, he watched Simon's lips move and concentrated on the words, the syllables, and sentences that built the suspense the author intended. When Simon reached the last page, it was five-thirty in the morning and Javier was stunned into silence.

Falling quiet, Simon closed the book, set it aside, and fell back onto his bed lengthwise. Javier chewed his thoughts, absently watching Simon watch the ceiling. Only when the kitchen clock rang in the quarter-hour did either of them speak.

"Sun-up in forty-five minutes." Simon rolled his head to the side to meet his pal's gaze, but Javier's face was red and his mouth a straight line. Simon sat up and threw his legs over the side of the bed. "What? Is something wrong?"

Javier clenched his jaw, losing the battle with the words that wanted so badly to exit. Rakum were not permitted to speak of mortal abstracts. There was no religion among the Brethren, yet something deep inside of him was proving stronger than the ancient tenets of his people. He looked into Simon's bright blue eyes and took a deep breath, ready to relinquish the fight. Leaning forward, he took his longtime donor by the forearm that he normally drew blood from and asked him point blank. "Will you tell me about God?"

There. It was out, and Javier was mortified. His people did not hold such frivolous and foolish notions. To do so would contradict the Ten Fathers, as well as the Elders assigned to educate them to adulthood. To do so would nullify his own deity, of which he had always been certain.

Until now.

Simon rubbed his eyes. "Sure. I mean, I never said anything before because I thought you weren't interested in that stuff. Do you want me to start from the beginning?"

"No," Javier sighed, sensing the unpleasant nudge of the sun nearing the horizon. He was disappointed that he would have to leave without finishing what he had started, but his time was up. "I'll come back tomorrow. Same time."

"I'll be here," Simon replied softly.

Javier nodded, stood, and turned for the closed bedroom door.

"Um, you didn't want..." Shyly, Simon lifted his forearm as well as his eyebrows.

Javier held up his hand. "Forget about it. I'll see you tomorrow." Simon's face fell, and Javier turned to leave. The kid's blood would ease his discomfort, but he had made his choices and tonight's preoccupation with the novel had erased any interest in a buzz.

Javier jogged the two blocks to his own residence. Once home and preparing to bed down, he thought about the characters from the novel and about the question he had asked Simon at the last. Mostly, he thought about the answer and what it might mean for him, his future, and that of his entire race. It meant *something*, but what? Had any of his brethren read the story? Did it move anyone else and wake something hidden deep inside of them? Was it ultimately going to be a bad thing that he peeked into the human concept of a Creator-God?

Javier slept fitfully and longed for the evening. To finish what he had started. Perhaps to learn about a God he had never known existed, one that would care for him and give him purpose. Ironically, he never knew he desired those things until he sat and listened to that silly woman's book.

Beth Rider's book.

4 *Don't Bother to Scream*

Beth left the room dark and collapsed face down on the hotel bed. She had no energy to even turn on a lamp. She'd spent the last two days and most of both evenings in various bookstores signing novels for her readers. Her left hand was numb from the effort, but for the most part, each book signing had been a joy. Only the dark maniac at Buckhead Books left a sour taste in her mouth. She had put him out of her mind, but now, she shivered at the recollection of the hellish encounter.

Beth flipped onto her back, still lying long-ways across the king-sized bed. A furtive movement to her right, beyond the glow of the tiny nightlight caught her attention and she sat up. She was not alone.

"Is this the way you watch your back?" a husky whisper rasped.

Beth jumped to her feet and lunged for the door. In three strides, the dark form across the room grabbed her from behind.

"Don't bother to scream…"

As one steel-like arm wrapped about her chest, smashing her breasts and holding her immobile, the other hand covered her mouth. Beth could not see her attacker, but it was definitely the tattooed monster from the night before. Beth prayed in her heart for help and went limp in her attacker's grasp.

"You're quite the nuisance. Have you any idea the trouble you're causing my people?" The voice paused and then continued in a guttural chortle that chilled Beth's soul. "I could handle this so many ways, Miss Rider. So many ways…"

Beth squeezed her eyes closed, unable to fathom the meaning of his accusation.

"Bel suggested I snuff you out, right here, right now." The stranger continued his one-way conversation in a gleeful tone. "But Tomás, on the other hand... his idea intrigues me. Want to know what Elder Tomás suggested?"

Beth did not respond praying for divine rescue.

"He said you'd make a delightful Rabbit." The giant smacked his lips. "Hah! I haven't marked a Rabbit since… *damn*… it's been a long time. Would you rather die now or become a Rabbit for my pups to play with?"

Beth didn't attempt to answer, even though the thought was moot with her mouth covered. She opened her eyes and trained them on the outline of the curtained window across the dark room.

"I'll tell you," the man continued in a teaching tone, as if she had asked a question. "A Rabbit is a toy for my pups. As in, a papa wolf finds a rabbit, marks it with his scent, turns it over to his pups, and they play with it. They practice their technique on it. They attack it again and again until it's worn out, or insane, or both."

The man paused and Beth worked to ignore the rising panic in her gut. Somehow, she knew he was not going to end her life, but whatever he had in mind was going to be horrible.

"Most of the time, Rabbits give up *long* before we're done with 'em. I wonder how long you'll last? I wonder how many of my pups you can entertain before you kill yourself?" The man's tone turned wistful as he finished his thought. Still with his left arm around her from behind and that hand pressed firmly over her mouth, his right arm disappeared and she felt his fingers against her throat.

"Hush, this might sting a bit…" His fingernail pressed into the curve of Beth's neck and continue inward until the skin split and blood trickled from the wound. "Are you the quiet type?"

He encircled the wound with his lips, his tongue pressing against her skin. Beth leapt into action. With mighty effort, she pushed off with all the strength she could muster. Although she didn't break free, the man's lips slipped away and she grunted with victory. As she struggled to free herself from the death grip on her face, the man secured her once more with his strong right arm. His left hand shifted and now covered her mouth *and* her nose.

"Can you wriggle free from this, you damn brat?"

Beth increased her attempts to break loose; she couldn't breathe and as panic crept in, all of her internal prayers ceased.

"I'm gonna mark you. It'll only take a minute if you're still."

Beth continued to strain, all of her senses on alert. She was no longer a rational being, but rather a wild animal fighting for her life. Just as she thought she might lose consciousness, the man's hand slipped off her nose and she took in a painful breath. The man shuffled her to the bed and forced her into a lying position, his looming shape taking a straddling stance over her. Beth's eyes grew wide in the dim room and she thrashed her entire body.

"Be still, you shit!" the monster hissed and again, closed her airway with a slight movement of his hand. His weight over her abdomen caused enormous pressure to her diaphragm and Beth grew still.

"Move again, I beg you," the man rasped. "I don't like you enough to explore what else you might be good for."

Horrified at the sexual threat, Beth quieted every muscle.

"That's right, heheh," he chuckled, his putrid breath falling on her cheeks. "You're too school-teacher for me, but I have *lotsa* brothers." The monster leaned down to sniff her hairline. "*Yeahhhh,* I can think of three or four who like them clean and innocent..."

"Mmmm!" Beth mumbled into his hand, her eyes vainly seeking his in the dim light.

"My mark will change you, make you smell like me, and then *all* of my pups will like you—*a lot.*" He stressed the last two words and held her gaze. "I am about to uncover your mouth. Hush, submit, and this will be over quickly. Understand?"

Beth nodded, her eyes bulging with terror. She didn't know what he intended to do, but he said it would be quick. Beth held on to that assurance and closed her eyes. The man's clammy hand slipped from her mouth and a warm liquid touched her lips, her tongue, and rapidly filled her mouth.

"I hope you're a swallower, Miss Rider," her gruff attacker jibed and pinched closed her nostrils. "All of it. *Swallow.*"

Beth's mind flashed to her novels. Her characters were forced to drink blood. Did this lunatic think he was a vampire? Is that what the entire ordeal was about? A psychotic and deluded fan of her novels acting out his fantasies? Even as her mind raced with comparisons, Beth swallowed to keep from choking. Immediately, the man removed his hands from her face and placed them down on the pillow to either side of her head. He looked upon her and now his fetid breath fell on her forehead.

"Wait for it..." the dark giant whispered.

He was waiting for something to happen and Beth opened her eyes to meet his glittering gaze. In the darkness, she saw only the reflection of the nightlight in her attacker's reddened eyes. Focusing on the general area of the man's scar, Beth worked to regain her composure. *What now?* Her mind was clearing, her morbid fear passing... What was he waiting for? Precisely five seconds later, Beth's stomach turned inside out.

"*Ugghhhhh!*" she groaned, writhing in pain beneath her monstrous enemy. The man did not cover her mouth as she twisted and strained beneath him, every nerve afire.

"*Sh-i-i-i-i-i-t...*" he chuckled, "you're hilarious."

Beth made an attempt to conceal her discomfort, and soon, the acid burn in her middle subsided. As she settled her frightened but angry gaze into that of her attacker, her pain melted into nausea and then disappeared altogether.

"You're freakin' hilarious," he said, spittle falling on her face.

Beth didn't respond and the dark brute sat up, still holding up his bulk just enough to prevent crushing her. His right hand dropped to her shirt, dragging heavily across her breasts.

"*Ehhhh,* so tender; my pups are going to be thanking me forever," he muttered. With one last lewd pass, he put both palms to his thighs and looked upon her. "Do you have any idea what just happened?"

Beth only glared, unsure of what she should say and unsure of whether or not she could control her tongue if she spoke.

"Mad little bunny," the man chuckled and patted the top of her head. "My mark is on you and that makes you a Rabbit. Now I'm releasing you into the world so my pups can hunt you down. No matter where you go, they'll seek you out. Did you know that a wolf can sniff out a rabbit from as far away as a mile? My pups' senses are far greater than that and you will smell like steak roasting on an outdoor grill. You know how wonderful that smells? *Mmmmm.*"

He paused for Beth to respond, but again she refused.

"All of my brethren will want a shot at you. A juicy new Rabbit is a rarity they will exploit to the max and in every way imaginable."

As numbness seeped up her spinal cord, Beth realized she was losing consciousness. She watched the silhouette of the big man as he crawled away and then stood.

"Let's see…where is it?"

He reached for her purse on the nightstand. Through heavy eyelids, she watched him locate her wallet and pluck out a plastic card that glinted in the low light. Beth whimpered as he dropped the purse beside her, her driver's license in his possession. Beth's head swam. She was done fighting, but the monster spoke again and she made an attempt to comprehend.

"I like to know where my Rabbits are headed. Montgomery, Alabama? I have some pups *'round them parts.*" He spoke the last few words in a put-on Southern accent. "They haven't seen a Rabbit in a *long* time," he laughed to himself with a shake of the head. "My favorite lieutenant's in Montgomery; he'll find you first. You won't like him; he's horny and hungry *all the time.*"

Chuckling, the man backed toward the door and wiggled his fingers in Beth's direction.

"Sleep now, Rabbit. But tomorrow..." He opened the door and bright light spilled in from the hallway. "You better start running." And he was gone.

Beth tried to be thankful she was alive, but numbness overtook her brain and she slipped away, falling into a deep sleep. In her dreams, she was running and staying out of reach of the wolves.

Just barely.

5 *No Donation Tonight*

Javier's bunkmate opened a vein for him before he left. As a result, when he arrived at Simon's, he was comfortable and ready to listen. Dietrich was an amicable fellow that Javier had been saddled with ten years ago. Elder Roman expected him to teach the rabid Rakum a little couth, but so far, Dietrich showed little sign of amending his wild-child ways.

Simon answered the door dressed for bed, a surprised but pleased look on his movie-star face.

"Hey, I was afraid you got busy with something else." Simon led him into the house, apologizing. "I'd already gone to bed. We got the place to ourselves. Bart's out of town for the week."

Bart was the reason they usually met in Simon's bedroom,

but Javier stopped in the den without heading for the back of the house.

"We can sit in here. There'll be no donation tonight."

"Oh..." Simon padded barefoot back into the living area and watched his guest settle into the sofa. "How about some water?"

"No, sit down. Tell me more about the God in that novel."

Simon sighed and collapsed into the recliner to Javier's left and kicked open the footrest. "Okay, but I'm no expert." Simon nodded when Javier urged him again. "The *whole universe* was created by one God, *the* God. All of the other gods and goddesses are fairy tales that man created because he couldn't control the real God. Get it? Over time, Man worked it out so he could be the *creator of god*. Make sense?"

"Is this what you believe?"

"Sure."

Javier was surprised at Simon's noncommittal answer. "What else? What's He like?"

"Oh, that's easy. God is all about judgment and rules, limits and parameters. He is *holy*—whatever the flip that means—and He thinks humans need to be holy, too. In the old days, the humans He made turned out to be all wicked and despicable, so God decided to make a nation of people who would worship only Him. That was when Israel was born..."

"The country? Or the race—the Jews?" Javier tried to follow, but so far, Simon's story was more far-fetched than the fiction novel that started their conversation.

"The Jewish people."

"Aren't you Jewish?"

Simon shrugged. "God created *my* people. And *we* were given all these laws and promises and stuff. And one day, He's supposed to come and take His earthly kingdom back into His control. Then there will be peace on earth forevermore." Seemingly done, Simon rubbed his chin.

Javier responded with a tiny shake of his head. "Wait. He'll come *back?* Where is He now?"

"Oh, sorry," Simon said and cleared his throat. "You really

don't know any of this." Javier held his face static and waited for the youngster to continue. Simon grinned. "God is everywhere, He's a spirit. The rabbis say that eventually, God will send us a mighty King to establish His throne in Jerusalem and the whole world will know the God of Israel is the one true God." Simon chuckled, but Javier was dead serious.

"And the preacher in your novel followed this God?"

"Uh, well..." Simon cleared his throat. "That character was a Christian. And Christians think Jesus is God. I don't know much about that stuff."

"But the novel is filled with characters that follow this Jesus..."

Simon lifted both hands, palms out. "What? Like I could tell you anything more? I was raised by an irascible aunt whose entire contribution to teaching me of my heritage was to show me how to get a good deal at the market. I'm telling you what I remember from shul, and that's like a lifetime ago. Religion is a drag."

Puzzled, Javier asked, "You don't care about this God that you say created you especially for Him? If you believe all this stuff, how can you dismiss it so easily?"

Simon scratched his head and offered a half-hearted grin. "I never think about it. I mean, I don't hang out with religious Jews and I've never met a Christian I could tolerate." Simon shrugged apologetically and his smile faded.

"How would one go about learning more? What would happen if we talked directly to God, like the preacher in the story? Do you think He'd listen, I mean, if He's up there?" Javier realized as he spoke that he *knew* there was a God. Somehow, he'd come to the realization without consciously doing so. He dropped the disclaimers. "Can I speak to Him without Him calling me first?"

Simon shrugged. "Sure. You can pray to Him, ask Him anything you want." Simon reached for a large hardbound book on the side table on his right. Flipping it open, he shuffled through the pages looking for a specific passage. "I dug this out for you. It's my bar mitzvah Tanakh.[11] Let's see..."

Javier watched him, his mind pondering what questions he might ask the Creator, and of course, if he'd receive a reply. The Rakum Elders spoke telepathically with the Ten Fathers, but for the rest of them, if they had larger questions, they turned to the Elders. Javier cleared his mind; sometimes Elder Roman read his thoughts and it would be better to keep the God-search to himself.

"Here it is," Simon said, bringing Javier out of his thoughts. "I always liked this one. It says, 'Call to Me and I will answer you and tell you great and mighty things that you do not know.'[12] How about that? Call to Him. I think it's that easy."

"What's He called? Just God?" Javier sat up from his position on the couch.

"Ummm," Simon stuttered and leafed through his book. "He has dozens of names. I guess if I was you, I'd just call Him God. I think if He's the real God, He's the only one that'll answer."

Javier chuckled. "Got it. Can I borrow that?"

Simon handed the Tanakh over and yawned. "Keep it as long as you like. They say those are His actual words."

"I'll see what happens." Javier stood, the heavy book under his arm. "How about the Rider novel. Are you done with that one? I'd like to read it myself."

Simon reached to the counter and grabbed the novel. "Sure. Keep it."

"Thanks." Javier caught the tossed book. "I'm shoving off. Thanks for everything."

"Oh, okay." Simon stood up. "When will I see you again?"

Javier sighed and shook his head, distracted by his plans for the evening discovering more about Simon's God.

"Come on, Javier," the youngster whined. "This is twice in a row."

"Let me work on this and I'll call you. This is going to

---

[11] Collection of Old Testament Scriptures given when he came of age at thirteen.

[12] Jeremiah

sound crazy, but…" Javier was about to stop himself, but didn't. "I think God is calling me. Does that sound crazy?"

Simon shook his head, his eyes to the side. "No. That's what He does. He's pokin' me, too, since we've been talking." Simon looked up then and stepped closer. "Just call me later, okay? Promise?"

Javier nodded and squeezed the youth's shoulder briefly before making a hasty exit. He reached the house in record time and headed down to the basement, prepared to begin reading about—and hopefully *listening* to—God.

6 *A Perfect Match*

Jesse Cherrie opened his eyes in time to watch Atlanta fade into his past. Every Tuesday at sundown, he left his comfortable apartment in New York City for JFK, hopped a 747 to Atlanta, and then a regional jet to Montgomery, Alabama. Most Rakum used the Rakum-owned NCJ, but Jesse preferred comfort, and the human jets had the best amenities. So he headed south once a week to check his holdings in the southern companies and of course, to visit Jack Dawn's favored lieutenant, Michael Stone.

Jesse and Michael went *way* back, practically to the beginning. Raised in the same lair-house and paired up by the group proctor, they were a perfect match. With Michael's natural brawn and Jesse's mystical gifts, there was nothing they couldn't accomplish together. Delivered to Elder Dawn for Ritual training, they were made tough and successful, having graduated at the head of their class over a century ago. Since then, they had settled into separate and comfortable lives, co-existing with the cattle that populated the planet, enjoying what mankind had to offer in the way of luxury and comfort.

…Well, Michael's not so much into the luxury…

Jesse sucked his teeth and pictured his pal's boring house,

considered his boring job, and his pitiful bank balance. Rakum grunts worked as hard as mortals to earn a living wage, but where Jesse learned to multiply money on the Stock Market, Michael pursued work more in tune with his natural military leanings. Making barely $50K a year, he kept the humans in line as a law enforcement officer. Jesse grinned to himself; Michael seemed satisfied which was all that mattered.

Jesse increased the volume on his iPhone. It wasn't so much the music, but the distraction. He had an hour-long flight ahead and preferred being left alone. Because he purchased both seats, Jesse set his briefcase in the aisle seat and turned his attention to the music.

As he nodded his head with the beat, he thought about the night ahead. Maybe Michael would join him for a night on the town. Last week they'd gone to a bar frequented by twenty-somethings sipping dainty cocktails and fruity wine-coolers. What Michael saw in the place, Jesse couldn't fathom. Well-known for his sexual appetite, Mike probably liked looking at the girls. But none of them were touchable and none were reliably alone. The one woman that maybe, just *maybe,* could have been convinced to sneak into the back with Mike for a snuggle ended up causing quite a stink.

Jesse glanced around the cabin, everyone was minding his or her own business. He closed his eyes and allowed the previous adventure to roll back. Michael Stone was fun to watch, especially when aroused by a potential buzz or provoked by a drunk idiot. The night in question, they enjoyed both extremes.

"Her," Michael had whispered, inclining his head toward a female at the opposite end of the bar. Jesse looked her over; she was petite and gentle-looking, like an elementary school teacher. Mike loved those—the meek little kittens. Jesse shook his head. He preferred his women confident, sexy, and a little frightening.

When Michael didn't make a move, Jesse comically

widened his eyes. "Well? Go ahead. I'm not your daddy."

Mike grinned, hopped off his stool, and strolled the length of the bar. Jesse sipped his beer and watched the show. If his friend succeeded (which he most assuredly wouldn't in such a place), he would get her to either come to his car, or go behind the establishment where Mike would swoon her for her blood. A handsome Rakum lieutenant such as his friend should have no trouble. So far, Michael had game. The tiny thing smiled and nodded. Then she laughed into her hand when he made an idiotic joke. Jesse finished his beer and almost ordered a second when the woman slid off her stool and put her hand on Michael's arm.

"You have got to be shitting me..." Jesse sent to his mind. Michael was a miserable telepath, but read Jesse well enough. His friend grinned and sent him a wink. Jesse followed with his eyes as they headed for the front exit. Only when another patron approached from behind and roughly grasped Michael's shoulder did things go sour. Jesse grinned; so the woman had a date, and Michael loved besting bullies.

"Hey, asshole!" the rude man shouted, not nearly as drunk as he was pretending. "You got some nerve!"

The man balled a fist as Mike's new lady friend scampered away, her eyes huge. Mike dodged the man's ridiculously-aimed jab and lifted his hands in surrender, smiling like the hulky oaf he was.

"Hey, man, chill out. What's your problem?" he said as the angry guy reared back to swing again, shouting expletives. Michael caught the fist as it entered his space and held it, careful not to break any bones. "Fella, fella," he cooed, "chill."

Mike outweighed the man by fifty pounds and stood at least an inch taller. Jesse shook his head when his friend shot him an amused look.

"Don't hurt him," Jesse sent telepathically and with his mouth, which was unnecessary. Both of them would do whatever it took to avoid contact with the mortal authority.

Michael released the man's hand and the guy lunged into his torso, grabbed him around the waist, and tried in vain to wrestle him to the ground. Mike stood in place with his arms sticking out and looked at the other patrons with humor in his gaze.

"Hey, fella, I apologize—whatever you're mad about, I'm sorry," Michael said loud enough for everyone to hear. The crowd had grown four deep and Jesse finally left his stool to better keep his eye on the show. Finally, someone who knew the brawler struggled into the fray, attempting to stop the fight. The attacker still had Michael around the middle when Jesse reached them.

"Let's go, Mike," he said aloud and his friend lifted both hands, showing his palms.

"This man is in love with me," he said and laughed. "Not my type, but he's plenty cute."

Mike's teasing further stoked the guy's fire. Jesse intuited from the jilted lover that he would not soon give up his attack and he looked Mike in the eye. *"You'll have to end it."*

Mike chuckled and playfully squeezed the man's shoulder. "Hey, little fella, would you like to come home with me? I'll put a guy like you to work right away," Mike said over his attacker's head.

The brawler shoved violently away and shouted, "I'LL SHOW YOU LITTLE!" The man whipped out a pocketknife that he pointed with practiced ease. Jesse tensed, but needn't have. Without pause, Mike disarmed him with a painful slap to his wrist.

The man bellowed his anger and Jesse overheard the words, "Call the cops." It didn't matter who said it. *"Time to go..."* he sent Mike and stepped behind the angry gentleman. Jesse carefully grasped the mortal by the neck and pulled him back several feet. He flailed his arms and Jesse handed him off to some of the other patrons, arms straight and head back, as one might hand over a wild animal. He then took Michael's elbow and pulled him out of the bar.

He almost got the girl and he almost got arrested.

Jesse chuckled at the memory and shook his head. Michael Stone was and always had been a fun companion, but tonight, they'd try somewhere new. Another song ended and in the break, someone clucked for his attention. Jesse opened his eyes and turned to the aisle, pulling out the ear bud on that side.

"I'm sorry to disturb you, sir, but we've had a little accident two rows back. Would you be so kind to allow this passenger to sit with you for a few minutes while we clean her seat?" It was the short blonde flight attendant who'd seated him earlier with a gigantic smile.

Jesse made an irritated noise as he pulled his case out of the seat to tuck under his knees. Blondie smiled, all dimples, blushing bright pink, and stepped aside for another person to pass. He was rearranging his case when she stepped in, so the first thing he saw was a toe-to-knee cast. The woman maneuvered carefully into the space, crutches, purse, and briefcase making the job a truer challenge. When she collapsed into the seat, Blondie left them alone.

"I'm sorry to barge in on you like this."

The woman stuck out her hand and Jesse shook without yet looking up, easily masking his distaste. He didn't welcome physical contact, but to fit the role he played, shaking with them was expected.

"My neighbor spilled his coffee in my seat when I stepped out to the restroom. How he could be so clumsy, I'll never know."

Jesse nodded his head and offered her a tight smile, still looking aside. If he could survive the intrusion for ten minutes without getting to know the woman, that would suit him best.

"I notice you wear your watch on the right. Are you left-handed?"

Jesse stifled a sigh. "Yes."

"I thought so," she replied, and held up her right hand to show that on her slender wrist dangled an expensive and feminine Rolex. Jesse nodded, appreciating her taste in watches, as he wore the same brand and she had already noticed the coincidence. She readied to make more small talk and he prepared for it, now allowing himself to study her eyes, her face, her mouth. Why not? She had barged into his private world and thus became fair game to scrutiny.

The woman's copper-colored hair was cropped close and spiked with product and she looked at him with confidence in her bright hazel eyes. Because of an organizational emblem on her purse strap, Jesse surmised that she was a tennis player and maybe a pro by the looks of her athletic build. Today she was dressed in a business suit, dark gray slacks, matching blazer, and a low-cut deep red silk shirt. A diamond and white-gold tennis racket adorned her lapel and her briefcase was similar to Jesse's. She made a comment about it as soon as she noticed his interest. He nodded and she launched into more conversation.

"I am buying a restaurant in Birmingham. Is that where you're headed?"

Jesse smiled and shook his head. As he expected, he'd spent enough time with the woman—a good four minutes, sitting close enough to touch—that he wanted to try her out. She wasn't wearing a wedding ring, which was a good first sign.

"No, Montgomery," he offered, slowly taking in her figure in such a way that she would notice. Without any obvious offense to his brazenness, she waited until his eye landed on her injured leg and placed her hand on her bare knee, just above the plaster.

"I was rear-ended last week." She rearranged the folded pants leg that made way for the cast and when Jesse met her eyes, she was watching him the way he was watching her. As far as she knew.

"What's your name?"

"Oh, sorry," the woman laughed and put her knee hand now to her breast, knowing Jesse would follow with his eyes. "Kelly Jacobs. Where are my manners?"

Jesse smiled wider and she blushed. He had her now. "Jesse Compton. Nice to meet you, Kelly." It was an alias he used often with women. Jesse Cherrie was a man you could Google. Jesse Compton was nobody he knew.

The woman accepted the name and batted her eyelashes as she looked away. They were so easy, and he was the luckiest Rakum he knew. Unlike Michael who situated regular blood donors all over town, Jesse had only two where he lived. He preferred to pick up his dinner on the fly. The variety and excitement gave him more satisfaction, which was of course his main goal.

Blondie returned just then and offered to help Kelly Jacobs back to her seat. Jesse held up his hand and invited her to stay.

"Oh, thank you, Jesse," she cooed with a coy smile.

Jessie sent the irritating tot away, relaxed into his seat, and stretched his legs. The tennis pro watched his every move, as he knew she would, and he could see he was her type.

"When we land in Montgomery, will you join me for a drink?" Jesse asked, giving her a glimpse of his killer smile. She interpreted his gaze as a come-on and blushed again. Jesse waited until she consented with a tiny nod. She played innocent, but she'd been around.

Jesse listened to her small-talk with one ear and the end of the Moody Blues album in the other, his plans for the night set: a much-deserved drink with a consenting female followed by a fun Tuesday night clubbing with Michael Stone. Jesse smiled at his fortune.

Ebook readers, read on for 99 cents. The paperback is priced as low as the printer will allow. We want you to love it as we do!

More Praise for Rabbit: Chasing Beth Rider

"I absolutely love it when an author can take a myth or legend and weave them neatly and efficiently into a brilliant and original tale. This book is definitely not simplistic in nature. Ms. Maze gives us a fast-paced plot with many twists and turns, not just in the action, but also for the mind. *Rabbit: Chasing Beth Rider* will grab your attention from the first page and will not let go until the end, and maybe not even then. Enjoy the chase!"

~ Stephanie Nordkap, *Bestsellersworld.com*

Maze takes us on a vampire journey with a one-of-a-kind twist! Rabbit is a fast-paced, action-packed, exciting vampire thriller. As an avid reader of vampire fiction, this gem unexpectedly has become one of my very favorites.

~ Marcia Freespirit, CEO, *JimSam Inc. Publishing*

Please sign up for Ellen's newsletter to be alerted of all new releases and freebies. Link:
https://dl.bookfunnel.com/z0c7dpe1am
Or at the CONTACT link at www.ellencmaze.com
Or by clicking "Follow" on Amazon.

[i] Matthew 6:9-13 (NIV)
Our Father in heaven, hallowed be your name, your kingdom come, your will be done, on earth as it is in heaven. Give us today our daily bread. And forgive us our debts, as we also have forgiven our debtors. And lead us not into temptation, but deliver us from the evil one

www.ingramcontent.com/pod-product-compliance
Lightning Source LLC
Chambersburg PA
CBHW060814120626
46557CB00001B/213